Suspended Sentences

Suspended Sentences: Three Novellas

PATRICK MODIANO

TRANSLATED FROM THE FRENCH BY
MARK POLIZZOTTI

YALE UNIVERSITY PRESS ■ NEW HAVEN & LONDON

A MARGELLOS
WORLD REPUBLIC OF LETTERS BOOK

The Margellos World Republic of Letters is dedicated to making literary works from around the globe available in English through translation. It brings to the English-speaking world the work of leading poets, novelists, essayists, philosophers, and playwrights from Europe, Latin America, Africa, Asia, and the Middle East to stimulate international discourse and creative exchange.

Yale University Press books may be purchased in quantity for educational, business, or promotional use. For information, please e-mail sales.press@yale.edu (U.S. office) or sales@yaleup.co.uk (U.K. office).

Set in Electra and Nobel types by Tseng Information Systems, Inc. Printed in the United States of America.

CONTENTS

Introduction: Missing, by Mark Polizzotti vii

Afterimage 1

Suspended Sentences 61

Flowers of Ruin 131

INTRODUCTION : MISSING

Mark Polizzotti

A feeling of indirection pervades many of Patrick Modiano's writings, and the three short novels in this volume are no exception. For all the specificity of detail—locations catalogued with loving precision, particular casts of light and shadow—one can't escape a sense of haziness, as if everything were shrouded in gauze or viewed through a Vaselined lens. The narrative voice adds to this impression, the protagonists often placing themselves just to the side of the situation they're describing. Like the prose in which they couch their stories, these narrators maintain a slight remove, as if full engagement with one's surroundings carried the threat of great pain, or mortal danger.

Readers familiar with Louis Malle's film *Lacombe Lucien* (1974), for which Modiano co-wrote the screenplay, will recognize this disengagement: it's the same unconsciousness that lets the title character drift into the world of French fascism, as if by accident. In the novellas included here, a similar diffidence colors the author's efforts in *After-image* to sort out his memories of the photographer Jansen, and the attempts by Patoche, the ten-year-old hero of *Suspended Sentences*, to penetrate the dubious adult world in which he and his brother live. Even the somewhat more skeptical protagonist of *Flowers of Ruin* is stymied by his inconclusive pursuit of the elusive Pacheco.

What becomes clear as we read these books is that the inconclusiveness of the pursuit is central to the story—indeed, *is* the story. Modiano's narrators seem fatally drawn to individuals who are uncommonly vague about themselves and their situation, people whose ability to engage the writer's emotional investment—and, one senses, to cause him harm—stands in inverse proportion to the amount of reliable information he's able to garner about them. Each of these novellas turns around a gap, a center that cannot hold: the nebulous Pacheco, the taciturn Jansen (for whom, in turn, the departed Robert Capa and Colette Laurent open a breach), and, for little Patoche, the figure of Annie, she of the bobbed hair, leather jacket, and exotic blue jeans, at once big sister and preadolescent crush, the main actor in a play of bewildering dialogues, entrances, and exits. It's as if each of these figures held the key to a great conundrum, as if they alone could bring everything into focus, but never do. Then again, perhaps this is intentional, for as Modiano confesses elsewhere, "The more obscure and mysterious things remained, the more interested I became in them. I even looked for mystery where there was none."

As befits the wistful undertone of these narratives, their setting is mainly a world gone by. Time and again we're reminded that a particular Parisian building or neighborhood was later razed to make room for something else, or are given a privileged introduction to an obscure nook of the city, usually near the outskirts, that harks back to earlier decades: the Hameau du Danube, the Poterne des Peupliers . . . One could easily read these novellas as a three-part love song to a Paris that no longer exists, or that most people's eyes do not see. Despite the action's contemporary setting and the frequent references to bright sunlight, we find ourselves plunged into the atmosphere of Marcel Carné's fog-drenched films, Edith Piaf's smoky laments, and Brassaï's nocturnal photographs. And, fittingly as well, the geography is more often than not the working-class neighborhoods of the city's northern quarters, or Saint-Germain-des-Prés before it became overrun with tourists and new money. The periphery, the zone, the no-man's-land where people stay just outside the law to get by: this is the territory of these novellas.

Few French writers have evoked Paris with as much fondness and nostalgia as Modiano. Baudelaire comes to mind, glowering with dis-

approval at the newly Haussmannized boulevards as he memorial-
izes the "swarming city, city filled with dreams" (for while "the city
scape / Is quick to change, less so the human heart"). So does Aragon,
the Paris peasant, conserving the gallerias of the second arrondissement and their alluring, defunct storefronts. Modiano's fictions offer
a connoisseur's excavation of the capital, a romance of lost itiner-
aries, such as his detailed re-creation in *Flowers of Ruin* of Urbain
and Giselle T.'s possible routes from Paris to the suburban town of Le
Perreux; or the lists—how these books do love lists!—of the sites on
which the Jansen of *Afterimage* trained his camera; or the resurrec-
tion, in *Suspended Sentences*, of the ill-defined "zone where Neuilly,
Levallois, and Paris all blended together," whose "streets were wiped
off the map when they built the *périphérique*, taking with them all
their garages and their secrets."

Although published separately over a period of five years, the
novellas in this volume have remarkable coherence, even if that coherence was unintentional. Modiano's comment for a French omnibus edition of his novels applies just as well here: taken together, he
says, those books "form a single work. . . . I thought I'd written them
discontinuously, in successive bouts of forgetfulness, but often the
same faces, the same names, the same places, the same sentences
recur from one to the other."

The resulting impression is of a self-contained world in which figures move and evolve but remain fundamentally similar, as if in a
less grandiose version of Balzac's *Comédie humaine*, a less buffoonish
commedia dell'arte, or Wes Anderson's ensemble-cast tragicomedies.
People reappear at unexpected moments, like those vaguely recognized characters one sees around the neighborhood. Coincidences
occur, sometimes remarked upon, sometimes passing unnoticed. It's
as if everything in Modiano's books, including the books themselves,
were governed by the six proverbial degrees of separation.

Among the recurrences one will find in these pages, there is the older woman who shows the preadult narrator some rare kindness (Annie in *Sentences*, the Danish girl in *Flowers*), only to be snatched away by someone more age-appropriate (often wearing a glen plaid suit). There is Pacheco, the great enigma, who intersects with the mystery of the T.'s in *Flowers of Ruin*, and who also makes a cameo appearance in the novel *Honeymoon* (1990). There is the "Rue Lauriston gang" (known to history as the Carlingue), part band of thieves, part Gestapo auxiliary, whitewashing its actions with a false patina of respectability. There is the black marketeer and collaborationist Eddy Pagnon, cryptically associated with Modiano's father. And there is the primal scene of the father's wartime arrest as an undocumented Jew by the French police, his liberation by that same Pagnon before he can be deported to a camp—and, in the background, the moral ambiguities of the Occupation and the indelible stain they have left on French history. This episode, which reappears, with variants, in all three books (though in *Afterimage* the father's role is played by Jansen), and in several others besides, is one of two central knots in Modiano's writing, like a trauma that can be recounted over and over but never exhausted. The other is the childhood death of his kid brother, Rudy; but of that pivotal event we hear no more than a whisper.

The temptation, when reading Modiano's fictions, is to assume they are slices of autobiography. Understandably so: alongside the repetition of nodal scenes, there are numerous correspondences between the personal histories of his storytellers (named Patrick, or its diminutive Patoche, and born, like him, in 1945) and the known facts of the author's own life. A number of these concordances were made explicit—unless they, too, were more invention—in his 2005 memoir *Un pedigree*. In it, one finds that Modiano's mother, like that of Patoche in *Sentences*, was an actress frequently away on tour, and that his father, Albert, like his fictional avatars, lived in the "murky world of secret dealings and the black market, in which he circulated by force of circumstance." (Both Jansen and Pacheco, by age as well as evasiveness, could be seen as paternal stand-ins.) The house in which young Patrick and Rudy lived for a while was located at 38 Rue du Docteur-Kurzenne in the suburb of Jouy-en-Josas, and corresponds exactly to the description of the house on "Rue du Docteur-Dordaine" in *Sentences;* the real-life Annie who looked after the boys at their mother's request was named Suzanne Bouquerau. There was a Frede (the nickname of a certain Suzanne Baulé) who ran a nightclub, and a Jean D. (Jean Normand, alias Duval) who spent time in jail, and a ruined castle, and a Duvelz or Duveltz, and a Danish girl named Kiki who helped the teenage Modiano when he ran away from school . . .

Most of all, there is the reality of Albert Modiano's arrest and unexplained release and the disappearance of Modiano's beloved brother, about whom he writes in *Un pedigree:* "Apart from my brother, Rudy, his death, I think that none of what I'll relate here truly concerns me. I'm writing these pages the way one draws up a report or CV, simply as documentation and to have done with a life that wasn't my own." The father, keeper of heavy secrets that he took to the grave, secrets of which his son can uncover only shards; the brother, vanished prematurely, his death bleaching the author's childhood of its emotional reality: these are the true voids in Modiano's writing, the mystery that remains unsolved, the ghost who cannot be exorcised, of whom all the other fugitives and absentees in his books are but shades.

And still, it is important to remember that these are fictions—however closely their strands might be woven from Modiano's own past—and it seems apt to quote once more his remarks from the French omnibus edition, in which he characterizes his novels as "a kind of autobiography, but one that is dreamed-up or imaginary. Even the photographs of my parents have become portraits of imaginary characters. Only my brother, my wife, and my daughters are real." As for the other figures who lend their presence to these pages, "I used their shadows and especially their names because of the sound; for me, they were nothing more than musical notes."

With these notes, Modiano has composed a haunting trilogy of love and loss, pitch-perfect in its quiet determination to elucidate the riddles of human identity. Writing, at its best, is a process of discovery, a way of both piercing and preserving a mystery that, by nature, cannot be clarified. Looking back on his attempts to discover the truth about Pacheco, the evidence he has scrupulously compiled, the narrator of *Flowers of Ruin* reflects: "Without fully realizing it, I began writing my first book. It was neither a vocation nor a particular gift that pushed me to write, but quite simply the enigma posed by a man I had no chance of finding again, and by all those questions that would never have an answer."

Note on the Translation

Generally speaking, and despite the ambiguities in his narrative strategy, Modiano's prose style is straightforward and clear—by which I do not mean simple—and I have aimed above all to preserve that limpid quality in this translation. His titles are another matter. While a direct translation worked perfectly well for *Flowers of Ruin* (*Fleurs de ruine*), and even allowed me to retain the whiff of Baudelairean spleen, this was not the case with *Remise de peine*—literally, a stay of sentence, but also a deferral of pain. By titling the English version *Suspended Sentences*, I hope to have kept both the sense of punishment delayed and the dual resonance by introducing a hint of the writer that young Patoche will eventually become.

Chien de printemps required the most liberty. The title—literally "dog of spring," figuratively an expletive along the lines of "rotten spring" or "miserable spring"—refers to Jansen's exclamation ("Goddamn spring"), but also to the actual dog that appears at the end of the book and to the season in which the action occurs. More allusively, the "dog in spring" could be the protagonist himself, sniffing after Jansen to learn his secrets, listless like an abandoned pet after the photographer's departure. One possibility that occurred to me was "bitch of a spring," but this neither captured the tone of the relationship nor was a convincing expletive (or, for that matter, a good title). The "dog days" fall in the wrong season, and plays on the word "hound" just seemed silly. Ultimately I decided to forgo the original altogether and concentrate on what this novella seemed most to be about: a retrospective attempt to *see*, an exercise in hindsight, an afterimage.

AFTERIMAGE

For Dominique

> Doorbells, dangling limbs, no one comes this far,
> Doorbells, swinging gates, a rage to disappear
> No dog has his day
> When the master's gone away
>
> —Paul Eluard

I met Francis Jansen when I was nineteen, in the spring of 1964, and today I want to relate the little I know about him.

It was early morning, in a café on Place Denfert-Rochereau. I was there in the company of a girl my age, and Jansen was at a table facing ours. He was watching us and smiling. Then, from a bag placed next to him on the imitation leather bench, he pulled out a Rolleiflex. I barely realized he'd trained his lens on us—that's how quick and casual his movements were. He used a Rolleiflex, but I couldn't say much about Jansen's technique or the papers he printed on, which infused all his photos with their particular light.

On the morning we met, I remember asking him, out of politeness, what he considered the best kind of camera. He shrugged his shoulders and admitted that, all things considered, he preferred those small black plastic cameras you can buy in toy stores, the kind that squirt water when you press the trigger.

He treated us to coffee and asked us to be his models again, but this time out in the street. An American magazine had hired him to illustrate an article on Paris youth, and he'd chosen the two of us, simple as that: it was easier and would go faster. And even if they weren't satisfied back in the States, it didn't matter: he just wanted to get this bread-and-butter assignment over with. We left the café and walked in the sun, and I heard him mutter with his slight accent:

"Goddamn spring."

A reflection he must have repeated many times that season.

He had us sit on a bench, then he posed us in front of a wall shaded by a row of trees, on Avenue Denfert-Rochereau. I've kept one of those shots. My girlfriend and I are sitting on the bench. To me it's as if they were other people, not us, because of the years that have passed, or maybe because of what Jansen saw through his lens, which we wouldn't have seen in a mirror at the time: two anonymous teenagers lost in Paris.

We went with him to his studio on Rue Froidevaux, a few steps away. I sensed he was apprehensive about being alone.

The studio was on the ground floor of an apartment building, and you entered it directly from the street. A large room with white walls, at the back of which a small flight of stairs led up to a loft. A bed took up the entire space of the loft. The only furnishings were a gray sofa and two armchairs of matching color. Next to the brick fireplace, three brown leather suitcases stacked one on top of the other. Nothing on the walls. Except two photos. The larger one was of a woman, a certain Colette Laurent, as I would learn. On the other, two men — one of whom was Jansen, younger — were sitting side by side in a shattered bathtub, among some ruins. Despite my shyness, I couldn't help asking Jansen about them. He'd answered that it was he, with his friend Robert Capa, in Berlin, in August 1945.

Until that day, I'd never heard of Jansen. But I knew who Robert Capa was, having seen his photos of the Spanish Civil War and read an article about his death in Indochina.

Years have passed. Rather than clouding the image of Capa and Jansen, they've had the opposite effect: the picture is much sharper in my memory now than it was that spring.

On the photo, Jansen looked sort of like Capa's double, or rather, like a little brother that the latter had taken under his wing. As much as Capa — with his dark brown hair, dark gaze, and the cigarette dangling from the corner of his lips — exuded brashness and joie de vivre, so Jansen — blond, skinny, light eyes, timid, melancholic smile — looked ill at ease. And Capa's arm resting on Jansen's shoulder was not merely friendly. It was as if he were holding him up.

We sat on the armchairs and Jansen offered us whiskey. He went to the back of the room and opened a door that led to a former kitchen, which he'd turned into a darkroom. Then he came back toward us.

"I'm awfully sorry, there isn't any more whiskey."

He sat a bit stiffly, legs crossed, at the very end of the sofa, as if he were only visiting. My girlfriend and I didn't try to break the silence. The room, with its white walls, was very light. The two chairs and the sofa were placed too far from each other, creating a feeling of emptiness. It was as if Jansen had already stopped living there. The three suitcases, whose leather reflected the sunlight, suggested imminent departure.

"If you're interested," he said, "I'll show you the photos when they're developed."

I had jotted down his phone number on a cigarette pack. Besides, he'd added, he was in the book. Jansen, 9 Rue Froidevaux. DANton 75-21.

At times, it seems, our memories act much like Polaroids. In nearly thirty years, I hardly ever thought about Jansen. We'd known each other over a very short period of time. He left France in June of 1964, and I'm writing this in April 1992. I never received word from him and I don't know if he's dead or alive. The memory of him had remained dormant, but now it has suddenly come flooding back this early spring of 1992. Is it because I came across the picture of my girlfriend and me, on the back of which a blue stamp says *Photo by Jansen. All rights reserved*? Or for the simple reason that every spring looks the same?

Today the air was light, the buds had burst on the trees in the gardens of the Observatoire, and the month of April 1992 merged by an effect of superimposition with the month of April 1964. The memory of Jansen pursued me all afternoon and would follow me forever: Jansen would remain someone I'd barely had time to know.

Who can tell? Someone else will write a book about him, illustrated with the pictures he'll find. There's a series of small black paperbacks devoted to famous photographers: why not one about him? He deserves it. In the meantime, it would make me glad if these pages rescued him from oblivion—though that oblivion is his own doing, deliberately sought.

I think I should set down the few biographical facts I've managed to piece together: He was born in 1920 in Antwerp and he barely knew his father. He and his mother were of Italian nationality. In 1938, after several years spent studying in Brussels, he left Belgium for Paris. There, he worked as an assistant to several photographers. He met Robert Capa, who in January 1939 brought him to Barcelona and Figueras, where they followed the exodus of Spanish refugees toward the French border. In July of that same year, he covered the Tour de France with Capa. When war was declared, Capa offered to take him to the United States and obtained two visas. At the last moment, Jansen decided to stay in France. He spent the first two years of the Occupation in Paris. Thanks to an Italian journalist, he worked for the photo services of the magazine *Tempo*. But despite this, he was picked up during a raid and interned as a Jew at the Drancy transit camp. He stayed there until the day the Italian consulate managed to have its citizens freed. Then he took refuge in the Haute-Savoie and waited out the rest of the war. Back in Paris, he was reunited with Capa and accompanied him to Berlin. During the following years, he worked for Magnum. After Capa's death and that of Colette Laurent—the woman friend whose portrait I'd seen on the wall of his studio—he withdrew further and further into himself.

I feel somewhat awkward giving these details, and I can imagine how embarrassed Jansen would be if he saw them set down here in black and white. He was a man of few words. He did everything he could to be forgotten, including leaving for Mexico in June 1964 and completely dropping out of sight. He often told me, "When I get there, I'll send a postcard so you have my address." I waited for it in vain. I doubt he'll ever come across these pages. If he were to, then I'd receive that postcard, from Cuernavaca or somewhere else, with just these words: "Be quiet."

But no, I wouldn't receive a thing. I only have to look at his photos to rediscover the quality he possessed in art as in life, which is so precious but so hard to acquire: keeping silent. One afternoon I'd paid him a visit and he'd given me the picture of my girlfriend and me on the bench. He'd asked what I was planning to do with my future, and I'd answered, "Write."

That activity struck him as "squaring the circle"—the exact phrase he'd used. Indeed, writing is done with words, whereas he was after silence. A photograph can express silence. But words? *That* he would have found interesting: managing to create silence with words. He had burst out laughing.

"So, are you going to try? I'm counting on you. But most of all, don't lose any sleep over it . . ."

Of all the punctuation marks, he told me, ellipses were his favorite.

I asked him about the pictures he'd been taking for nearly twenty-five years. He pointed to the three leather suitcases, stacked one on top of the other.

"I put everything in there . . . If you're interested . . ."

He stood up and nonchalantly opened the topmost suitcase. It was full to the brim and a few pictures fell out. He didn't even bother picking them up. He rummaged around inside, and other photos spilled from the valise and lay scattered on the floor. He finally fished out a volume and handed it to me.

"Here . . . I did this when I was about your age. This must be the last remaining copy in the world. It's yours . . ."

It was a copy of *Sun and Snow*, published in Geneva, Switzerland, by the publisher La Colombière in 1946.

I picked the prints up off the floor and put them back in the suitcase. I said it was a shame to leave them all helter-skelter like that, that someone should organize and catalogue the contents of the three suitcases. He looked at me in surprise.

"You won't have time . . . I have to leave for Mexico next month."

Still, I could try to finish by then. I had nothing else to do during the day, since I'd dropped out of school and had earned a little money—enough to live on for a year—from the sale of some furniture, paintings, carpets, and books from an abandoned apartment.

I'll never know what Jansen thought of my initiative. I think he probably didn't care. But he gave me the spare key to the studio so I could come work when he was out. I was often all alone in the large room with its white walls. And every time Jansen came home, he looked startled to see me. One evening as I was sorting the photos, he took a seat on the sofa and watched me without a word. Finally, he asked, "Why are you doing this?"

That evening, he suddenly seemed intrigued by my activities. I'd answered that these pictures had documentary value, since they bore witness to people and things that no longer existed. He had shrugged.

"I can't stand to look at them anymore . . ."

His voice took on a serious tone I'd never heard him use.

"You understand, kid, it's like every one of those pictures was a kind of guilty conscience for me . . . It's better to start from scratch . . ."

When he used an expression like "squaring the circle" or "start from scratch," his accent became more pronounced.

He was forty-four years old at the time and today I understand better his state of mind. He would have liked to forget "all that," come down with amnesia. But he hadn't always felt this way. Indeed, on the back of every photo, he had written a detailed caption with the date he'd taken it, the place, the name of the person depicted, and even a few additional remarks. I pointed this out.

"I must have been as obsessive as you back then . . . But I've changed a lot since . . ."

The telephone rang, and he said what he always did:

"Tell whoever it is I'm not here."

A woman's voice. She had already called several times. A certain Nicole.

I was always the one who answered. Jansen didn't even want to know who'd called. And I pictured him there alone, sitting at the far end of the sofa, listening to the rings as they followed each other in the silence.

Sometimes the doorbell rang. Jansen had asked me never to answer, because "people" — he used that vague term — might come in and wait for him in the studio. Every time it rang, I hid behind the sofa so that I couldn't be seen through the picture window from the street. It suddenly felt as if I'd entered the studio illegally and I was afraid the people ringing, spotting a suspicious presence inside, would go report it to the nearest precinct.

The "last square" — his term — was coming to hound him. And in fact, I'd noticed it was always the same people who phoned. That woman Nicole, and also "the Meyendorffs," as Jansen referred to them: the man or woman asked that he "call them back right away." I jotted down the names on a piece of paper and gave him the messages, despite his complete lack of interest. I recently found, among other souvenirs, one of those pieces of paper bearing the names of Nicole and the Meyendorffs, along with the two other people who often rang up: Jacques Besse and Eugène Deckers.

Jansen called them the "last square" because the scope of his relations had gradually narrowed over the preceding years. I finally realized that Robert Capa's death, and Colette Laurent's not long afterward, had opened a void in his life.

I didn't know much about Colette Laurent. She figured in a number of Jansen's photos, but he only spoke of her indirectly.

Twenty years later, I discovered that I'd met this woman in my childhood and that I could have told Jansen something about her myself. But I hadn't recognized her in the photos. All I had kept of her was an impression, a scent, dark brown hair, and a gentle voice asking me if I studied hard in school. Certain coincidences risk passing unnoticed; certain people have appeared in our lives on several occasions without our realizing it.

One spring, even earlier than the one when I met Jansen, when I was about ten years old, I was walking with my mother and we met a woman at the corner of Rue Saint-Guillaume and Boulevard Saint-Germain. We strolled together for a while, and she and my mother talked. What they said is lost in the mists of time, but I remembered the sundrenched sidewalk and her name: Colette. Later, I heard she'd died in dubious circumstances during a trip abroad, and it had struck me. I had to wait several decades for a link to emerge between those two moments of my life: the afternoon on the corner of Rue Saint-Guillaume and my visits to Jansen's studio on Rue Froidevaux. Just half an hour on foot from one point to the other, but such a long distance in time . . . And the link was Colette Laurent, about whom I know almost nothing, except that she'd been very important to Jansen and that she'd lived a turbulent life. She had come to Paris when she was very young, from a distant province.

Not long ago I tried to imagine her first day in the capital and I felt sure it was much like today, with long stretches of clear sky alternating with sudden showers. Wind from the Atlantic shakes the tree branches and turns umbrellas inside out. Pedestrians huddle in doorways. You can hear the seagulls crying. Sunlight glistens on wet sidewalks near the Quai d'Austerlitz and on the walls around the Jardin des Plantes. She walked for the first time through a city sluiced out and laden with promise. She had just arrived at the Gare de Lyon.

Here's another memory of Colette Laurent, from my childhood. In the summer, my parents would rent a tiny cottage in Deauville, near Avenue de la République. Colette Laurent had shown up unexpectedly one day. She looked very tired. She shut herself in the small living room and slept for two days straight. My mother and I spoke in whispers so as not to disturb her.

On the morning when she finally woke up, she offered to take me to the beach. I walked next to her beneath the arcades. When we reached the Clément Marot bookstore, we crossed the street. She put her hand on my shoulder. Instead of continuing straight on to the beach, she dragged me to the Hôtel Royal. At the entrance, she said, "Go ask the man at the front desk if he has a letter for Colette."

I walked into the lobby and, stammering, asked the concierge if he had "a letter for Colette." He didn't seem surprised by the question. He handed me a very large, very thick brown envelope on which someone had written her name in blue ink: COLETTE.

I exit the hotel and hand her the envelope. She opens it and looks inside. Still today I wonder what it contained.

Then she walks with me to the beach. We sit on deckchairs, near the Soleil bar. At that time of day, there's no one there but us.

I had bought two red Clairefontaine notebooks, one for me, the other for Jansen, so that I could catalogue his photos in duplicate. I was afraid he'd misplace the fruit of my labors en route to Mexico, out of indifference or carelessness, so I decided to keep a copy. Today it makes me feel odd when I leaf through the pages: it's like reading a very detailed catalogue of images that don't exist. What became of them, when we're not even sure what became of their maker? Did Jansen bring the three suitcases with him, or did he destroy it all before leaving? I had asked him what he was planning to do with those suitcases and he'd said that they were weighing him down, and that he especially didn't want any "excess baggage." But he didn't offer to leave them with me in Paris. At best, they've now more or less rotted away in some suburb of Mexico City.

One evening when I'd stayed in the studio later than usual, he came home just as I was copying over in the second notebook what I'd already written in the first. He had leaned over my shoulder:

"That's painstaking work, kid . . . Aren't you tired?"

I sensed a touch of sarcasm in his voice.

"If I were you, I'd go further . . . I wouldn't stop at just two note-books . . . I'd make an alphabetical index of every person and place that appears in those photos . . ."

He smiled. I was disconcerted. I felt he was laughing at me. The next day, I started compiling an alphabetical index in a large register. I was sitting on the sofa, among the piles of photos that I took from the suitcases a few at a time, and I wrote by turns in the two notebooks and in the register. This time, Jansen's smile froze and he looked at me in amazement.

"I was joking, kid . . . And you took me seriously . . ."

But I wasn't joking. I had taken on this job because I refused to accept that people and things could disappear without a trace. How could anyone resign himself to that? After all, Jansen had shown the same concern. Reading over the index, which I still have, I notice that a lot of his pictures were scenes of Paris or portraits. On the backs of the earliest ones he had written down where they'd been taken; otherwise it would have been hard for me to identify most of them. They showed steps, curbs, gutters, benches, shredded posters on walls or barricades. No taste for the picturesque, but simply his own eye, an eye whose sad and attentive expression I can still recall.

Among the photos, on a sheet of letter paper, I had discovered some notes in Jansen's hand, titled "Natural Light." It was for an article that a film journal had requested, since he'd worked pro bono as a technical adviser to several young directors in the early sixties, teaching them how to use floodlights like American newsreel cameramen during the war. Why had those notes impressed me so deeply at the time? Since then, I've come to realize how hard it is to find what Jansen called "natural light."

He had told me that he shredded street posters himself to uncover the ones hidden beneath the newer strata. He pulled the strips down layer by layer and photographed them meticulously, stage by stage, down to the last scraps of paper that remained on the billboard or stone wall.

I had numbered the photos in chronological order:

325. *Fence on Rue des Envierges*
326. *Wall, Rue Gasnier-Guy*
327. *Steps on Rue Lauzin*
328. *Passerelle de la Mare*

329. *Garage on Rue Janssen*

330. *Site of the old cedar tree at the corner of Rue Alphonse-
Daudet and Rue Leneveux*

331. *Slope of Rue Westermann*

332. *Colette, Rue de l'Aude*

I drew up a list of individuals whose portraits Jansen had taken.
He had approached them at random, in the street, in cafés, while
taking a walk.

My walk, today, took me as far as the Orangerie in the Jardins du
Luxembourg. I crossed the shaded area under the chestnut trees, near
the tennis courts. I stopped at the bowling ground. Several men were
playing a match. My attention was caught by the tallest of them, who
was wearing a white shirt. One of Jansen's pictures came to mind, on
the back of which was written a caption that I'd copied onto my list:
Michel L., Quai de Passy. Date unknown. A young man in a white
shirt resting his elbow on a marble mantelpiece in very bright light.

Jansen clearly recalled the circumstances surrounding that photo.
He was broke, and Robert Capa, who had connections, found him an
easy, well-paying assignment. He had to go to an American woman's
home on the Quai de Passy, with all the necessary equipment for
studio portraits.

Jansen had been surprised by the size and luxuriousness of the
apartment, the multiple balconies. The American woman was around
fifty, still dazzling, but old enough to be her young French compan-
ion's mother. He was the one Jansen was there to photograph. The
American woman wanted several photos of this "Michel L.," in the
style of Hollywood headshots. Jansen had set up the spotlights as if he
were accustomed to this type of work. And for six months he'd lived
off the money he'd earned from those photos of "Michel L."

The more I watched the man preparing to toss his ball, the more
I was sure I recognized "Michel L." What had struck me about the
picture were the eyes, close to the surface and slanted toward the

temples, which gave "Michel L." a strange look, as if he had compound eyes with an abnormally wide angle of vision. And the man before me had the same slanted eyes and profile as "Michel L." The white shirt only accentuated the resemblance, despite his gray hair and pasty skin.

The playing ground was surrounded by a metal edging, and I didn't dare cross that boundary and disturb the game. There was more than forty years' distance between the "Michel L." whom Jansen had photographed and the bowls player today.

He walked to the edging while one of his friends pitched the ball. He stood with his back to me.

"Pardon me . . ."

My voice was so blank that he didn't hear.

"Pardon me . . . There's something I'd like to ask you."

This time I had spoken much more clearly, articulating each syllable. He turned around. I planted myself firmly in front of him.

"Did you ever know the photographer Francis Jansen?"

His strange eyes seemed to stare at something off on the horizon. "How's that?"

"I wanted to know if you ever had your picture taken by the photographer Francis Jansen."

But a short distance away, an argument had broken out among the others. One of them came toward us.

"Lemoine, it's up to you now."

Suddenly it was as if he was looking past me, or right through me. Nonetheless, he said, "I'm sorry . . . I have to go bowl . . ."

He got into position and pitched the ball. The others cheered. They crowded around him. I didn't understand how the game worked, but I think he'd won the match. In any case, he had completely forgotten about me.

These days, I regret not having kept any photos from the suitcases. Jansen wouldn't even have noticed. Moreover, if I'd asked, I'm sure he would have given me as many as I wanted.

And besides, you never think at the time to ask the questions that will elicit confidences. And so, out of discretion, I avoided bringing up Colette Laurent. I regret that too.

The only photo I kept was in fact one of her. I hadn't yet remembered that I'd met her a dozen years earlier, but her face must have reminded me of something.

The photo is captioned *Colette, 12 Hameau du Danube*. When daylight lasts until 10 P.M. because of the time change, and the traffic noise has died down, I have the illusion that all I'd need do is return to those faraway neighborhoods to find the people I've lost, who had never left: Hameau du Danube, the Poterne des Peupliers, or Rue du Bois-des-Caures. Colette is leaning against the front door of a private townhouse, hands in the pockets of her raincoat. Every time I look at that picture, it hurts. It's like in the morning when you try to recall your dream from the night before, but all that's left are scraps that dissolve before you can put them together. I knew that woman in another life and I'm doing my best to remember. Maybe someday I'll manage to break through that layer of silence and amnesia.

Jansen came to the studio less and less often. At around seven in the evening, he would call:

"Hello . . . Is that you, Scribe?"

That was the nickname he'd given me. He asked if anyone had come to the door and if he could stop by without fear of intruders. I reassured him. Just a phone call from the Meyendorffs this afternoon. No, no sign of Nicole.

"Okay, Scribe, then I'll be right over. See you in a bit."

Sometimes he'd call back half an hour later:

"Are you sure Nicole's not around? Is it really safe to come over?"

I had stopped working and waited for him a little longer. But he never showed up. So then I left the studio. I walked down Rue Froidevaux, skirting the cemetery. That month, the trees had regrown their leaves and I was afraid Nicole was hiding behind one of them, lying in wait for Jansen to return home. If she saw me, she'd come up and ask where he was. She might also be lurking on the corner of one of the little streets that spilled onto the left-hand sidewalk and could follow me at a distance in hopes that I'd lead her to him. Back then, because of what Jansen said, I considered Nicole a threat.

One afternoon, she came to the studio when Jansen was out and on an impulse I answered the door. It bothered me, always having to tell her over the phone that Jansen wasn't there.

When she saw me in the half-open doorway, an expression of startled anxiety flashed in her eyes. Perhaps she thought Jansen had left for good and a new tenant was now living there.

I quickly reassured her. Yes, I was the one who answered the phone. Yes, I was a friend of Francis's.

I invited her in and we both took a seat, she on the sofa and I in an armchair. She had noticed the two notebooks, the large register, the open suitcases and piles of photographs. She asked if I was working for Francis.

"I'm trying to catalogue all the pictures he's ever taken."

"Ah, I see . . . You're right, that's a good idea."

There was an awkward pause. She broke the silence.

"I don't suppose you know where he is?"

She'd said it in a tone that was at once timid and rushed.

"No . . . He comes here less and less often . . ."

She took a cigarette case from her bag, opened it, then shut it again. She looked me in the eye.

"Couldn't you speak to him on my behalf, ask him to see me one last time?"

She laughed briefly.

"Have you known him long?"

"Six months."

I wanted to know more. Had she shared a life with Jansen?

She cast curious glances around her, as if she hadn't been here in an eternity and wanted to see what had changed. She must have been around twenty-five. She had brown hair and very pale eyes, perhaps light green or gray.

"He's a strange guy," she said. "He can be very sweet and then, from one day to the next, he disappears . . . Has he done that with you, too?"

I answered that I often didn't know where he was.

"For the last two weeks he's refused to see me or even take my calls."

"I don't think he's trying to be cruel," I said.

"No . . . No . . . I know . . . It happens now and again. He has these absences . . . He goes into hiding . . . And then he resurfaces."

She took a cigarette from her case and offered it to me. I didn't want to tell her that I didn't smoke. She took one as well. Then she lit mine with a lighter. I took a puff and coughed.

"How do you explain that?" she suddenly asked.

"What?"

"That strange need of his to go into hiding?"

I hesitated a moment, then said, "Maybe it's because of events in his past . . ."

My gaze had fallen on the picture of Colette Laurent hanging on the wall. She was about twenty-five as well.

"I must be keeping you from your work . . ."

She was about to get up and leave. She would no doubt hold out her hand and give me another futile message for Jansen. I said:

"No, no . . . Stay a bit longer . . . You never know, he could be back any minute now."

"And you think he'll like finding me here?"

She gave me a smile. For the first time since she'd entered the studio, she was paying real attention to me. Until that moment, I'd been in Jansen's shadow.

"Will you take responsibility for that?"

"I'll take full responsibility," I told her.

"In that case, he might be in for a nasty surprise."

"No, not at all. I'm sure he'll be very glad to see you. He has a tendency to withdraw into himself."

I suddenly became talkative, to hide my shyness and embarrassment. She was staring at me with those pale eyes. I added:

"If someone doesn't twist his arm, he could end up going into hiding for good."

I closed the notebooks and register that were lying on the floor and stored the piles of photos in one of the suitcases.

"How did you meet him?" I asked her.

"Oh . . . By chance . . . Not far from here, in a café . . ."

Was it the same café on Denfert-Rochereau where my girlfriend and I had first met him?

She knit her eyebrows, which were brown and contrasted with her pale eyes.

"When I learned what he did for a living, I asked him to take some pictures of me. I needed them for work. He brought me here . . . And he took some beautiful shots of me."

I hadn't come across them yet. The most recent ones I'd catalogued were from 1954. Maybe he hadn't kept anything after that year.

"So if I've got this straight, he hired you to be his secretary?"

She was still staring at me with her transparent eyes.

"Not at all," I said. "He doesn't need a secretary anymore. These days he barely has a business to run."

The evening before, he'd invited me to dinner at a small restaurant near the studio. He was carrying his Rolleiflex. At the end of the meal, he had put it on the table and told me it was over, that he didn't want to use it anymore. He was giving it to me. I told him that was a real shame.

"You have to know when to quit."

He had drunk more than usual. During the meal, he had emptied a bottle of whiskey, but you could hardly tell: just a slight fog around the eyes and his speech was slower.

"If I keep at it, it will only give you more work for your catalogue. Don't you think that's enough as it is?"

I had walked with him to a hotel on Boulevard Raspail, where he'd taken a room. He didn't want to go back to the studio. "That girl," as he put it, might be waiting at the door; she was really wasting her time with "a guy like him."

She was sitting there, in front of me, on the sofa. It was already 7 P.M. and daylight was fading.

"Do you think he'll come today?" she asked.

I was sure he wouldn't. He would go dine alone somewhere in the neighborhood, then head back to his hotel room on Boulevard Raspail. Then again, he might call at any moment for me to meet him at a restaurant. And if I told him Nicole was here, how would he react? He'd immediately assume she'd pick up the extension. And then he'd pretend to be calling from Brussels or Geneva and would even agree to talk to her. He'd tell her his stay there might last for quite a while.

But the telephone didn't ring. We sat opposite each other in the silence.

"Can I wait for him some more?"

"As long as you like."

The room was sinking into shadow and I got up to put on the light. When she saw me reach for the switch, she said, "No . . . Please, no lights."

I went to sit on the sofa. I felt as if she'd forgotten my presence. Then she looked up at me:

"I live with someone who's very jealous and who's liable to come rap at the door if he sees the lights on."

I remained silent. I didn't dare suggest that I could simply answer the door and tell this potential visitor that there was no one else at the studio.

As if she had read my thoughts, she said:

"He'd probably just barge past you to see if I'm here . . . He might even punch you out."

"Is he your husband?"

"Yes."

She told me that Jansen had taken her to a neighborhood restaurant one evening. Her husband had spotted them by chance. He'd stormed up to their table and backhanded her across the face. Two slaps that had made the corners of her mouth bleed. Then he'd run off before Jansen could intervene. He had waited for them outside. He walked a good distance behind them, following them down the street, bordered by trees and endless walls, that cuts through the Montparnasse cemetery. She had gone into the studio with Jansen and her husband had stood planted for almost an hour in front of the door.

Since that misadventure, she figured, Jansen was having second thoughts about seeing her. Given how calm and cavalier he tended to be, I could easily imagine his discomfort that evening.

She explained that her husband was ten years older than she. He was a mime and performed in what they used to call "Left Bank" clubs. I saw him two or three times after that, prowling around Rue Froidevaux in the afternoon to catch Nicole leaving the studio. He gave me an insolent stare. Dark and fairly tall, with a romantic allure. One day I went up to him.

"Are you waiting for someone?"

"I'm waiting for Nicole."

Theatrical, slightly nasal voice. In his bearing and his gaze, he played on his slight resemblance to the actor Gérard Philippe. He was wearing a kind of black frock coat and a very long, unknotted scarf.

I'd said, "Which Nicole? There are so many Nicoles."

He had given me a disdainful look, then made an about-face toward Place Denfert-Rochereau, with an affected gait as if he were walking offstage, scarf floating in the breeze.

She looked at her wristwatch in the semidarkness.

"It's okay now, you can turn on the lights. It's safe now. He has to start his act at the Ecole Buissonnière."

"What's that?"

"It's a cabaret. He does two or three shows a night."

He went by the stage name Gil the Mime and he performed against a soundtrack of poems by Jules Laforgue and Tristan Corbière. He had had Nicole record the poems, so that it was her voice you heard every night as he moved around the stage in simulated moonlight.

She told me her husband was a real tyrant. He kept telling her that when a woman lived with an "artist," she should be devoted to him "body and soul." He erupted in jealous scenes over the flimsiest of pretexts, and that jealousy had become even more pathological since she'd met Jansen.

At around ten o'clock, he'd leave the Ecole Buissonnière for the Vieille Grille on Rue du Puits-de-l'Ermite, suitcase in hand. It contained his only prop: the tape recorder and the tapes on which his poems were recorded.

And where was Jansen, did I think? I told her I really had no clue. For a moment, just to appear interesting, I thought of telling her about the hotel on Boulevard Raspail, but I kept it to myself. She asked if I would walk her home. It was better if she got back before her husband. She spoke of him some more. Naturally, she no longer felt any respect for him, she found his jealousy and "artistic" pretensions ridiculous, but I could tell she was afraid of him. He always came home at eleven-thirty to make sure she was there. Then he went out again, to the last cabaret he performed in, an establishment in the Contrescarpe neighborhood. He stayed there until two in the morning and forced Nicole to accompany him.

We walked beneath the trees down Avenue Denfert-Rochereau and she plied me with questions about Jansen. I answered evasively: yes, he traveled a lot because of his work and he never let me know where he was. Then he'd show up unexpectedly, only to disappear again the same day. A real fly-by-night. She stopped and looked up at me:

"Listen . . . If he shows up at the studio someday, could you give me a call on the QT? I'll come right over . . . I'm sure he'll let me in . . ."

She took a scrap of paper from her raincoat pocket and asked if I had a pen. She jotted down her telephone number.

"You can call me at any time of day or night to let me know."

"What about your husband?"

"Oh . . . my husband . . ."

She shrugged. Apparently this didn't strike her as an insurmountable obstacle.

She tried to put off what she called "returning to prison" and we strolled a bit more through streets that today make me think of a kind of scholastic subdistrict: Ulm, Rataud, Claude-Bernard, Pierre-et-Marie-Curie . . . We crossed Place du Panthéon, sinister in the moonlight, which I never would have dared cross alone. In retrospect, the quarter seems to have been deserted as if after a curfew. Moreover, that evening from almost thirty years ago recurs often in my dreams. I'm sitting on the sofa next to her, so distant that I feel like I'm with a statue. The long wait has clearly petrified her. An early evening summer light bathes the studio. The photos of Robert Capa and Colette Laurent have been taken down from the wall. Almost no one lives here. Jansen has left for Mexico. And we keep on waiting for nothing.

At the foot of the Montagne Sainte-Geneviève, we entered a blind alley: Rue d'Ecosse. It had started to rain. She stopped in front of the last building. The entryway was wide open. She put a finger to her lips and pulled me into the foyer. She didn't turn on the hallway light.

There was a sliver of light beneath the first door to the left off the hallway.

"He's already here," she whispered in my ear. "I'm going to get the crap beaten out of me."

I was surprised to hear that word in her mouth. The rain fell harder and harder.

"I can't even lend you an umbrella . . ."

I kept my eyes fixed on the sliver of light. I was terrified he'd come out.

"You should wait here in the hall until the storm ends. My husband doesn't know who you are."

She squeezed my hand.

"If Francis ever comes back, you'll let me know right away—promise?"

She switched on the hall light and put her key in the lock. She glanced back at me one last time. She went in and I heard her call out in a shaky voice, "Hi, Gil."

The other kept silent. The door shut behind her. Before the hall light went out, I just had time to notice their mailbox, hanging on the corridor wall among the others. On it, in ornate red letters, were the words:

Nicole
and
Gil
Mime   Poet

The sound of furniture falling over. Someone slammed against the door. Nicole's voice:

"Leave me alone . . ."

It sounded as if she was struggling. The other was still silent. She let out a muffled cry, as if he was strangling her. I thought of intervening, but instead I stood frozen in the dark, under the entryway. The rain had already formed a puddle on the sidewalk in front of me.

She cried out, "Leave me alone!" louder this time. I was about to knock on the door when the sliver of light went out. After a moment, the creaking of bedsprings. Then sighs and Nicole's husky voice saying again, "Leave me alone . . ."

It kept raining while she emitted staccato whimpers and I heard the creak of the bedsprings. Later, the rain was no more than a kind of spittle.

I was about to walk out the entrance door when the hall light went on behind me. They were both in the hallway and he was carrying his suitcase in his hand. His left arm was around Nicole's shoulder. They walked by and she pretended not to know me. But at the corner she looked back and gave me a brief wave.

One sunny afternoon in May, Jansen had surprised me at my labors. I'd told him about Nicole and he'd listened, looking distracted.

"She's a nice girl," he'd said, "but I'm old enough to be her father..."

He didn't entirely get what it was her husband did for a living and, remembering the evening when he'd seen him slap Nicole in the restaurant, he again expressed surprise that a mime could be so violent. Personally, he imagined mimes as having very slow, gentle movements.

We'd gone out together and had barely taken a few steps when I recognized the silhouette stationed at the corner of the walled street that bisects the graveyard: Gil the Mime. He was wearing a black jacket and black trousers, with an open-necked white shirt whose wide collar covered his lapels.

"Well, well . . . There's a familiar face," Jansen muttered to me.

He waited for us to walk by him, arms folded. We continued down the opposite sidewalk and pretended not to notice him. He crossed the street and planted himself right in our path, legs slightly parted. He crossed his arms again.

"Think it's going to come to blows?" Jansen asked me.

We walked up to where he was standing and he blocked our way, hopping from foot to foot like a boxer about to throw a punch. I shoved him aside. His left hand landed on my cheek as if by reflex.

"Come along," Jansen said to me.

And he led me away by the arm. The other man turned toward Jansen:

"Hey, you! Shutterbug! What's your hurry?"

His voice had the metallic timbre and overly stressed diction of certain members of the Comédie Française. Nicole had told me he was also an actor and that he'd recorded himself on the soundtrack to his show, the last excerpt: a long passage from Alfred Jarry's *Ubu Roi*. He was quite attached to it—apparently, it was the purple passage and crowning touch of his act.

We kept walking toward Place Denfert-Rochereau. I looked back. In the distance, beneath the sun, I could make out only his black suit and brown hair. Was it because of the graveyard's proximity? There was something lugubrious about his silhouette.

"Is he following us?" Jansen asked.

"Yes."

Then he told me that twenty years earlier, on the day when he was caught in a police roundup coming out of the George-V metro stop, he'd been sitting in the subway across from a brown-haired man in a dark suit. At first he'd taken him for a regular passenger but, a few minutes later, the man was among the team of plainclothesmen who were bringing them in to the lockup, he and about ten others. He had vaguely sensed the man following him in the subway corridors. Gil the Mime, with his black suit, reminded him of that plainclothesman.

He was still following us, hands in his pockets. I heard him whistling a tune that used to terrify me when I was a child: "There Was a Little Ship."

We took a sidewalk table at the café where I'd first met Jansen. The other man stopped when he caught up to us and folded his arms. Jansen pointed at him for me.

"He's as clingy as that cop from twenty years ago," he said. "For all we know, maybe it's him."

The sun was blinding. In the harsh, shimmering light, a black spot was floating in front of us. It came closer. Now Gil the Mime stood out against the glare. Was he going to perform one of his shadow pantomimes for us, to a poem by Tristan Corbière?

He stood there, next to our table. Then he shrugged his shoulders and with an arrogant air strode off toward the Denfert-Rochereau metro stop.

"It's time for me to leave Paris," Jansen said. "This is all getting too tiresome and absurd."

The more I remember these details, the more I adopt Jansen's point of view. In the few weeks when I knew him, he considered people and things from a great distance, and all that remained for him were vague reference points and hazy silhouettes. And, through a kind of reciprocity, those people and things lost their consistency on contact with him. Could Gil the Mime and his wife still be alive somewhere? Try as I might to convince myself and imagine the following situation, I can't really believe in it: thirty years later, I run into them in Paris; the three of us have grown older; we sit at a sidewalk café table and calmly share our memories of Jansen and the spring of 1964. Everything that seemed so mysterious to me becomes clear and even ordinary.

Such as the evening when Jansen had gotten together with several friends in the studio, just before leaving for Mexico — a "farewell party," he said with a laugh . . .

Remembering that evening, I feel a need to latch onto those elusive silhouettes and capture them as if in a photograph. But after so many years, outlines become blurred, and a creeping, insidious doubt corrodes the faces. So many proofs and witnesses can disappear in thirty years. And besides, I had felt even at the time that the contact between Jansen and his friends had already loosened. He would never see them again and he didn't seem to mind. *They* were probably surprised Jansen had invited them at all, after not having heard from him in so long. Conversations started and almost immediately died. And Jansen seemed so absent, he who should have been the point in common for all those people . . . It was as if they'd found themselves by chance in the same waiting room. The small number of them only accentuated the malaise: four, sitting very far apart from one another. Jansen had set up a buffet, which added to the strangeness of the evening. Now and then, someone stood up and walked to the buffet to get a glass of whiskey or a cracker, and the others' silence enshrouded the event in an exceptional solemnity.

Among the guests at the "farewell party" were the Meyendorffs, a couple in their fifties whom Jansen had known for a long time: I'd catalogued a photo in which they figured in a garden with Colette Laurent. The man was dark, slim, with fine features, and wearing tinted glasses. He spoke in a very soft voice and was nice to me, even asking what I planned to do in life. He had been a doctor, but I don't believe he still practiced. His wife, a small brunette, with hair pulled back in a bun and high cheekbones, had the strict air of a former ballet instructor and a slight American accent. The other two guests were Jacques Besse and Eugène Deckers, whom I'd spoken to on the telephone several times in Jansen's absence.

Jacques Besse had been a talented musician as a young man. Eugène Deckers devoted his leisure time to painting and had renovated a huge loft on the Ile Saint-Louis.[1] Belgian by birth, he made a living playing supporting roles in English B movies, since he was bilingual. But I knew nothing of that at the time. That evening, I was content just to watch them without asking too many questions. I was at an age where one often finds oneself in strange company; all things considered, these people were no stranger than anyone else.

---

1. I later discovered that Jacques Besse had composed the music for Jean-Paul Sartre's *The Flies* and the film score for *Dédée d'Anvers*. The last addresses I was able to find for him were 15 Rue Hégésippe-Moreau, Paris 18, and Château de la Chesnaie, Chailles (Loir-et-Cher), tel.: 27.

Eugène Deckers had several exhibitions. He died in Paris in 1977. His address was 25 Quai d'Anjou, Paris.

Toward the end of the evening, the atmosphere relaxed. It was still light out and Eugène Deckers, trying to liven things up a bit, proposed that we all go have a drink outside, on the bench opposite the studio. We went out, leaving the door open. There were no more cars on Rue Froidevaux. We could hear the leaves trembling and the faraway rumble of traffic near Denfert-Rochereau.

Deckers was carrying a tray laden with aperitifs. Behind him, Jansen was dragging one of the studio armchairs, which he set in the middle of the sidewalk. He gestured for Mme de Meyendorff to have a seat. He was suddenly the Jansen of old, the one who had spent his evenings with Robert Capa. Deckers played the maître d', balancing the tray on his hand. With his dark, curly hair and pirate's face, one could easily imagine him taking part in those boisterous evenings Jansen had told me about, when Capa would cart him around in his green Ford. The awkwardness from earlier had lifted. Dr. de Meyendorff was seated on the bench next to Jacques Besse and was talking to him in his soft voice. Standing on the sidewalk, holding their glasses as if at a cocktail party, Mme de Meyendorff, Jansen, and Deckers were having a conversation. Mme de Meyendorff ended up sitting in the armchair, in the open air. Jansen turned to Jacques Besse:

"Will you sing us 'Cambriole'?"

The song, written when he was twenty-two, had once made Jacques Besse's reputation. He had even been held up as leader of a new generation of musicians.

"No, I don't feel like it . . ."

He gave a sad smile. He had stopped writing music long ago.

Their voices now blended in the silence of the street: Dr. de Meyendorff's, very soft and very slow; his wife's, deeper; Deckers's, punctuated by great bursts of laughter. Only Jacques Besse, a smile on his lips, remained silent on the bench, listening to de Meyendorff. I stood a bit apart, watching the entrance to the street that cut through the cemetery: maybe Gil the Mime would show up and keep his distance, arms crossed, thinking Nicole was coming to join us. But no.

At a certain moment, Jansen came up to me and said, "So? Happy? It's beautiful out this evening . . . Life is just starting for you . . ."

And it was true: I still had all those long years ahead of me.

Jansen had spoken to me several times of the Meyendorffs. He had seen a lot of them after the deaths of Robert Capa and Colette Laurent. Mme de Meyendorff was a believer in the occult sciences and spiritualism. Dr. de Meyendorff—I've come across the calling card he gave me at the "farewell party": Doctor Henri de Meyendorff, 12 Rue Ribéra, Paris XVI, Auteuil 28-15, and Le Moulin, Fossombrone (Seine-et-Marne)—occupied his leisure time studying Ancient Greece and had written a short book on the myth of Orpheus.[2]

For several months Jansen had attended séances organized by Mme de Meyendorff. Their goal was to make the dead talk. I feel an ingrained distrust and skepticism toward this sort of activity, but I can understand why Jansen would turn to it in his time of affliction. One would like to make the dead talk; one would especially like them to come back for real, and not merely in our dreams where they stand beside us, but so far away and so absent . . .

From what he'd confided, he had known the Meyendorffs long before the time when they'd figured in the photo, in the garden with Colette Laurent. He'd met them when he was nineteen. Then the war had broken out. Since Mme de Meyendorff was American, she and her husband had set sail for the United States, leaving Jansen the keys to their Paris apartment and their country house, where he had spent the first two years of the Occupation.

I've often thought that the Meyendorffs would have been the people most likely to provide information about Jansen. When he

---

2. *Orphée et l'Orphéisme* by H. de Meyendorff (Paris: Editions du Sablier, 1949).

left Paris, I had finished my work: all the materials I'd gathered about him were in the red notebook, the alphabetical index, and the album *Snow and Sun*, which he'd been kind enough to give me. Yes, if I had wanted to write a book about Jansen, I'd have had to go see the Meyendorffs and take notes on what they said.

Some fifteen years ago, I was leafing through the red Claire-fontaine notebook and, discovering Dr. de Meyendorff's calling card in its pages, I dialed his phone number, but it was "no longer in service." The doctor wasn't listed in that year's phone book. To settle the matter once and for all, I went to 12 Rue Ribéra, where the concierge told me she didn't know anyone by that name in the building.

That Saturday in June, so close to summer vacation season, it was very warm at around two in the afternoon. I was alone in Paris, with the prospect of a long, idle day ahead of me. I decided to go to the other address on the doctor's card, in the Seine-et-Marne region. Naturally, I could have tried information to find out if a Meyendorff still lived in Fossombrone, and if so call him on the phone, but I decided I'd rather see for myself, on site.

I took the metro to the Gare de Lyon, then bought a ticket for Fossombrone at the window for the commuter trains. I had to change at Melun. The compartment I entered was empty, and I was practically giddy at the thought of having found a purpose to my day.

It was while waiting on the platform of Melun station for the branch line to Fossombrone that my mood shifted. The early afternoon sun, the few travelers, and the thought of visiting people whom I'd only seen once, fifteen years before, and who had probably either died or forgotten me, suddenly made everything seem unreal.

There were two of us in the small local train: a woman in her sixties, carrying a shopping bag, had sat down opposite me.

"Good lord, this heat . . ."

I was reassured at hearing her voice, but surprised that it was so clear, with a slight echo. The leather of the seats was burning hot. There wasn't a single area in the shade.

"Will we arrive in Fossombrone soon?" I asked her.

"It's the third stop."

She rummaged through her shopping bag and finally found what she was looking for: a black wallet. She kept silent.

I wished I could have broken the silence.

She got off at the second stop. The local started up again and I was gripped by panic. I was alone now. I was afraid the train would take me on an endless journey, gradually gathering more and more speed. But it slowed down and stopped at a small station with tan walls on which I read FOSSOMBRONE in dark red letters. Inside the station, next to the ticket windows, a newspaper stand. I bought a daily after making sure of the date and skimmed the headlines.

I asked the news dealer if he knew a house named Le Moulin. He told me to follow the main road out of the village and continue straight on to the edge of the forest.

The shutters of the houses on the main road were closed to ward off the sun. No one was outdoors, and perhaps I should have worried about being alone in the middle of this unfamiliar village. The main road now turned into a wide path lined with plane trees, whose leaves barely let the sun's rays filter through. The silence, the stillness of the leaves, the dapples of sunlight I walked on brought back the sensation of being in a dream. I again checked the date and the headlines on the newspaper I was holding, to keep me tied to the outside world.

On the left, just at the edge of the forest, stood a low surrounding wall and green wooden gate on which LE MOULIN was written in white paint. I stepped back from the wall and went across the path to get a better view of the house. It seemed to be composed of several farm buildings cobbled together, with nothing rustic about them: the balcony, the large windows, and the ivy climbing up the façade made them look like bungalows. The neglected garden was now just a clearing.

The surrounding wall made a right angle and continued for another hundred or so yards along a pathway that skirted the forest and led to several other properties. The one next to Le Moulin was a white villa shaped like a bunker with bay windows. It was separated from the pathway by a white fence and privet hedges. A woman in a straw hat was mowing the lawn and I was relieved to hear the hum of a motor break the silence.

I waited until she was near the entrance gate. When she saw me, she shut off the lawnmower. She took off her straw hat. A blonde. She came over and opened the gate.

"Does Doctor de Meyendorff still live at Le Moulin?"

I'd had trouble pronouncing those syllables. They sounded weird.

The blonde looked at me in surprise. My voice, my awkwardness, the sound of "Meyendorff" had something incongruous and formal about them.

"Le Moulin hasn't been lived in for a long time," she said. "At least not since I've been in this house."

"Is it possible to go inside?"

"You'd have to ask the caretaker. He comes three times a week. He lives in Chailly-en-Bière."

"You wouldn't know where the owners are, by any chance?"

"I think they live in the States."

In which case, there was a good chance it was still the Meyendorffs.

"Are you interested in the house? I'm sure it's for sale."

She had invited me into her garden and closed the gate behind me.

"I'm writing a book on someone who used to live here and I just wanted to see what the place was like."

Once again I felt as if I'd used too formal a tone.

She led me to the back of her garden. A fence marked the boundary with the neglected grounds of Le Moulin. There was a large hole in the fence and she pointed to it.

"It's easy to get to the other side . . ."

I couldn't believe it. Her voice was so gentle, her eyes so clear, she was being so thoughtful . . . She had moved closer to me and I suddenly wondered if I was doing the right thing prowling around an abandoned house, on "the other side," as she said, instead of staying with her and getting to know her better.

"While you're over there, would you mind lending me your paper?"

"With pleasure."

"I wanted to see what's on television."

I handed her the paper. She said:

"Take your time. And don't worry—I'll keep a lookout."

I slid through the hole in the fence and emerged into the clearing. I walked toward the house. As I moved forward, the clearing gave way to an unkempt lawn bisected by a gravel path. Up close Le Moulin looked as much like a bungalow as it had from the entrance gate. To the left, the main house extended into a chapel, on which the door had been removed and which was now just a storage shed.

The shutters on the ground floor were closed, as were the two green panels of a French window. Two tall plane trees stood about ten yards apart, and their intermeshed foliage formed a roof of greenery that reminded me of a mall in a southern town. The sun was beating down, and it felt noticeably cooler in the shade.

It was definitely here that Jansen had taken the picture of Colette Laurent and the Meyendorffs. I recognized the plane trees and, to the right, the ivy-covered well with its coping. In the red notebook, I had written, "Photo of the Meyendorffs and Colette Laurent in Fossombrone. Shadows. Spring or summer. Well. Date unknown." I had asked Jansen what year the photo was taken, but he'd only shrugged.

The house jutted out on the right and the shutters to one of the ground floor windows were open. I pressed my forehead against the glass. The sun's rays projected a dappled light onto the back wall. A painting was hanging there: Mme de Meyendorff's portrait. In a corner of the room, a mahogany desk behind which I could make out a leather armchair. Two similar armchairs near the window. Bookshelves on the right-hand wall, above a green velvet couch.

I wanted to break into that room, where bit by bit the dust of time had settled. Jansen must have sat on those armchairs often and I could imagine him, on some late afternoon, reading a book from the library. He had come here with Colette Laurent. And, later, it was no doubt in this office that Mme de Meyendorff had called upon the dead.

Next door, on the lawn, the blonde had gone back to work, and I heard the peaceful, reassuring hum of the motor.

I never went back to Fossombrone. And today, fifteen years later, I suppose Le Moulin has been sold and the Meyendorffs are finishing out their days somewhere in America. I haven't had any recent news of the other people Jansen had invited to his "farewell party." One afternoon in May 1974 I ran across Jacques Besse on Boulevard Bonne-Nouvelle, near the Théâtre du Gymnase. I'd held out my hand, but he hadn't noticed and had walked away stiffly, without recognizing me, his eyes vacant, wearing a dark gray turtleneck and several days' beard.

One night a few months ago, very late, I had turned on the television, which was showing an English detective program adapted from Leslie Charteris's *The Saint*, and I was surprised to see Eugène Deckers. The scene had been filmed in London in the 1960s, possibly the same year and same week that Deckers had come to the "farewell party." There, onscreen, he was crossing a hotel corridor, and I thought it really strange that one could pass from a world in which everything ended to another, freed from the laws of gravity, in which you were suspended for all eternity: from that evening on Rue Froidevaux, of which nothing remained except the fading echoes in my memory, to those several seconds captured on film, in which Deckers would cross a hotel corridor until the end of time.

That night, I had dreamed I was in Jansen's studio, sitting on the sofa as in the past. I was looking at the photos on the wall, and suddenly I was struck by the resemblance between Colette Laurent and my girlfriend at the time, with whom I'd first met Jansen—someone else of whom I'd long had no news. I convinced myself that she and

Colette Laurent were one and the same person. The distance of years had confused matters. They both had chestnut hair and gray eyes. And the same first name.

I left the studio. It was already dark out and that surprised me. I remembered that it was October or November. I walked toward Denfert-Rochereau. I was supposed to meet up with Colette and a few others in a house near the Parc Montsouris. We got together there every Sunday evening. And, in my dream, I was certain I'd find among the guests that evening Jacques Besse, Eugène Deckers, and Dr. and Mme. de Meyendorff.

Rue Froidevaux seemed to go on forever, as if the distances stretched to infinity. I was afraid of arriving late. Would they wait for me? The sidewalk was matted with dead leaves and I skirted the wall and the grassy embankment of the Montsouris reservoir, behind which I pictured the still water. A thought stuck with me, vague at first, then becoming clearer: my name was Francis Jansen.

The day before Jansen left Paris, I had arrived at the studio at noon to put away the photos in the suitcases. I had no reason to expect his sudden departure. He'd told me he wasn't going anywhere until the end of July. A few days earlier, I'd given him the second copies of the notebook and the inventory of images. At first he'd been hesitant to take them.

"Do you really think I need this right now?"

Then he had leafed through the index. He lingered on a page and sometimes uttered a name aloud, as if trying to recall the face that went with it.

"That's enough for today . . ."

He had snapped the index shut.

"You've done a fine job as a scribe. Congratulations . . ."

That last day, when he came into the studio and caught me putting away the photos, he congratulated me again:

"A true archivist . . . They should hire you at a museum."

We went for lunch at a local restaurant. He was carrying his Rollei-flex. After lunch, we walked along Boulevard Raspail, and he stopped in front of the hotel on the corner of Rue Boissanade, the one that stands alone next to the wall and trees of the American Center.

He stepped back to the curb and took several shots of the hotel façade.

"That's where I lived when I first came to Paris . . ."

He recounted that he'd become ill on his first evening here and had kept to his room for a good ten days. He'd been treated by an

Austrian refugee who was living in the hotel with his wife, a certain Dr. Tennent.

"I took a photo of him at the time."

I checked it out that same evening. As I'd indexed the photos in chronological order in the red Clairefontaine notebook, this one was mentioned at the top of the list:

> 1. *Doctor Tennent and his wife. Jardins du Luxembourg. April 1938.*

"But I didn't yet have a photo of the hotel . . . You can add it to your list."

He asked me to walk with him to the Right Bank, where he had to go pick up "something." At first he planned to take the metro at Raspail station, but, after seeing on the map that there were too many transfers to get to Opéra, he decided we'd take a taxi.

Jansen asked the driver to stop on Boulevard des Italiens, in front of the Café de la Paix, and he pointed to the sidewalk tables, saying:

"Wait for me here. I won't be long."

He headed toward Rue Auber. I paced up and down the boulevard. I hadn't been in the Café de la Paix since my father used to take me on Sunday afternoons. Out of curiosity, I went in to see whether the automatic scale on which we weighed ourselves back then was still in its place, just before the entrance to the Grand Hôtel. Yes, it was still there. And so I couldn't resist stepping onto it, sliding a coin in the slot, and waiting for a pink ticket to drop.

It felt odd to be sitting alone on the sidewalk of the Café de la Paix, where customers were crowding around tables. Was it the June sun, the roar of traffic, the foliage on the trees whose green formed such a striking contrast with the black of the façades, those foreign voices I heard from the neighboring tables? It was as if I, too, were a tourist, lost in a city I didn't know. I stared fixedly at the pink ticket as if it were the last object capable of attesting to and reassuring me of my identity, but the ticket only increased my malaise. It called to mind a part of my life so distant that I could barely relate it to the present. I ended up wondering if I was really the child who used to come here with his father. Numbness and amnesia gradually overcame me, like sleep on the day when I was hit by a van and they pressed an ether-soaked pad over my face. In another moment, I'd no longer even know who I was, and none of these strangers would be able to tell me. I tried to fight against the numbness, my eyes fixed on the pink ticket that said I weighed 168 lbs.

Someone tapped me on the shoulder. I looked up but the sun was in my eyes.

"You look pale . . ."

I saw Jansen only as a silhouette. He took a seat across from me.

"It's because of the heat," I stammered. "I think I was feeling faint . . ."

He ordered a glass of milk for me and a whiskey for himself.

"Drink that," he said. "You'll feel better afterward."

I sipped the ice-cold milk. Yes, little by little, the world around me regained its shapes and colors, as if I were adjusting a pair of binoculars to bring them into focus. Jansen, in front of me, looked at me kindly.

"Don't let it faze you, kid. I've fallen into my share of black holes too . . ."

A breeze was ruffling the leaves on the trees, and their shade felt cool as Jansen and I walked along the main boulevards. We had come to Place de la Concorde. We went into the gardens of the Champs-Elysées. Jansen took pictures with his Rolleiflex, but I scarcely noticed. He cast a furtive eye on the viewfinder, level with his waist. And yet I knew that each of his photos was perfectly framed. One day, when I'd expressed surprise at that feigned carelessness, he'd told me you had to "approach things gently and quietly or they pull away."

We had sat on a bench and, still talking, he stood up now and then and pressed the shutter as a dog passed by, or a child, or a ray of sunlight appeared. He had stretched out and crossed his legs and his head was lolling as if he'd dozed off.

I asked what he was shooting.

"My shoes."

Via Avenue Matignon, we entered Faubourg Saint-Honoré. He pointed out the building that housed the Magnum agency and suggested we have a drink in the café next door where he used to go with Robert Capa, back in the day.

We sat at a rear table, and again he ordered a glass of milk for me and a whiskey for himself.

"This is where I met Colette," he said suddenly.

I wanted to ask questions, talk about the few photos of her I'd indexed in the red notebook:

> *Colette, 12 Hameau du Danube*
> *Colette with an umbrella*
> *Colette, beach at Pampelonne*
> *Colette, steps on Rue des Cascades*

I finally said, "It's too bad I didn't know all of you at the time . . ."

He smiled at me.

"But you were still in diapers . . ."

And he pointed to my glass of milk, which I was holding in my hand.

"Wait a second . . . Don't move . . ."

He set the Rolleiflex on the table and pressed the shutter. I have that photo here next to me, with all the other ones he took that afternoon. My raised arm, my fingers clutching the glass, are sharply defined against the glare; in the background you can make out the open door of the café, the sidewalk, and the street bathed in summer light—the same light in which we walked, my mother and I, in my memory, alongside Colette Laurent.

■

After dinner, I walked him back to the studio. We made a long detour. He was more talkative than usual and for the first time he asked specific questions about my future. He was worried about what my living conditions would be. He mentioned the precariousness of his life in Paris when he was my age. Meeting Robert Capa had saved him; without that, he might not have had the courage to strike out in his field. Moreover, it was Capa who had taught it to him.

It was already past midnight and we were still chatting on a bench on Avenue du Maine. A pointer trotted alone down the sidewalk, rapidly, and came up to sniff us. It had no collar. It seemed to know Jansen. It followed us to Rue de Froidevaux, first at a distance, then it came up and walked alongside us. We arrived at the studio and Jansen felt in his pockets but he couldn't find his key. He suddenly looked exhausted. I think he'd had too much to drink. I opened the door with the spare he'd given me.

In the doorway, he shook my hand and said in a solemn tone:

"Thank you for everything."

He stared at me with a slightly clouded gaze. He closed the door before I had a chance to say that the dog had slipped into the studio behind him.

The next morning, I phoned at around eleven but there was no answer. I had used our prearranged signal: three rings, hang up, ring again. I decided to go over there to finish putting away the photos.

As usual, I opened the door with my spare key. The three suitcases had disappeared, along with the picture of Colette Laurent and the one of Jansen with Robert Capa that had been hanging on the wall. On the coffee table, a roll of film to be developed. I took it that afternoon to the shop on Rue Delambre. When I went back to get it a few days later, I discovered in the envelope all the photos Jansen had taken during our walk through Paris.

I knew that there was no longer any point in waiting for him.

I searched through the closets upstairs, but there was nothing in them, not a single article of clothing, not even a sock. Someone had removed the sheets and bedclothes, and the mattress was bare. Not one cigarette butt in the ashtrays. No more glasses or bottles of whiskey. I felt like a police inspector looking through the apartment of a man who'd been wanted for a long time, and I told myself it was useless, since there was no proof the man had ever lived here, not even a fingerprint.

I waited until five o'clock, sitting on the sofa, looking through the red notebook and the index. Apparently, Jansen had taken the second copies of the notebooks. Perhaps Nicole would ring at the door and I'd have to tell her that from now on we'd probably be waiting for Jansen in vain and that centuries from now, an archeologist would find the two of us mummified on the sofa. Rue Froidevaux would become an excavation site. At the corner of the Montparnasse cemetery, they'd find Gil the Mime turned into a statue, and they'd hear his heart beating. And the tape recorder, behind him, would still be playing a poem that he'd recorded in his metallic voice:

Demons and marvels
Winds and tides . . .

A question suddenly occurred to me: what had become of the pointer that had followed us the night before, the one that had slipped into the studio without Jansen realizing it? Had he taken it with him? Now that I think about it, I wonder whether the dog wasn't simply his.

I went back to the studio later, when evening was falling. A final spot of sunlight lingered on the sofa. Between those walls, the heat was stifling. I opened the bay window. I could hear the rustling of the trees and the footfalls of people walking in the street. I was amazed that the roar of traffic had stopped farther over toward Denfert-Rochereau, as if the feeling of absence and emptiness that Jansen left was spreading in concentric circles and Paris was gradually clearing out.

I wondered why he hadn't told me he was leaving. But those few signs were indicative of an imminent departure: the photo he'd taken of the hotel on Boulevard Raspail and the detour up to Faubourg Saint-Honoré to show me Magnum's old headquarters and the café he used to frequent with Robert Capa and Colette Laurent. Yes, he had made, in my company, a final pilgrimage to the places of his youth. At the back of the studio, the darkroom door was ajar. The afternoon when Jansen had developed the pictures of my girlfriend and me, the small light bulb had shone red in the dark. He stood in front of the developing tray with rubber gloves on. He had handed me the negatives. When we went back into the studio, the light of the sun had blinded me.

I didn't hold it against him. I even understood him so well . . . I had noticed in him certain ways of acting and certain character traits that had become familiar. He'd said to me, "Don't let it faze you, kid. I've fallen into my share of black holes too . . ." I couldn't predict the future, but thirty years later, when I'd become the same age as Jansen, I wouldn't answer the telephone either, and I would disappear, as he had, one June evening, in the company of a phantom dog.

Three years later, on a June evening that strangely enough was the anniversary of his departure, Jansen was very much on my mind. Not because of that anniversary, but because a publisher had just accepted my first book, and in the inner pocket of my jacket I had a letter announcing the news.

I remembered that at one point on the last evening we'd spent together, Jansen had expressed concern about my future. And today, they'd assured me that my book would soon be published. I had finally emerged from that period of vagueness and uncertainty during which I lived as a fraud. I would have liked it if Jansen had been around to share my relief. I was sitting at a café near Rue Froidevaux, and for an instant I was tempted to go call at the studio, as if Jansen were still there.

How would he have greeted that first book? I hadn't respected the instructions of silence he'd given me the day we'd spoken about literature. No doubt he would have deemed it much too indiscreet.

When he was the same age as I, he was already the author of several hundred photos, some of which composed *Sun and Snow*.

That evening, I flipped through *Sun and Snow*. Jansen had told me he wasn't responsible for the namby-pamby title, which the Swiss publisher had chosen himself, without asking his opinion.

As I turned the pages, I felt more and more what Jansen had been trying to communicate, and what he'd gently challenged me to suggest with the word *silence*. The first two images in the book bore the same caption: *At number 140*. They depicted one of those clusters of buildings on the outskirts of Paris on a summer's day. Nobody in the courtyard or in the doorways to the stairs. Not one silhouette in the windows. Jansen had told me that a friend his age had lived there, someone he'd known in the Drancy transit camp. When the Italian consulate had Jansen released, the friend had asked him to go to that address to let his relatives and girlfriend know how he was doing. Jansen had gone to number 140, but he'd found none of the people his friend had mentioned. He'd gone back again after the Liberation, in the spring of 1945. In vain.

And so, feeling helpless, he'd taken those photos so that the place where his friend and his friend's loved ones had lived would at least be preserved on film. But the courtyard, the square, and the deserted buildings under the sun made their absence even more irremediable.

The next images in the book dated from before the ones of number 140, since they'd been taken when Jansen was a refugee in the Haute-Savoie: expanses of snow, its whiteness contrasting with the blue of the sky. On the slopes were black dots that must have been skiers, a toy-sized ski lift, and the sun beating down on all of it, the same sun as for "number 140," an indifferent sun. Through that snow and that sun showed an emptiness, an absence.

Sometimes, Jansen took objects from very close up: plants, a spider's web, snail shells, flowers, blades of grass with ants bustling among them. One felt that he trained his gaze on something very specific to avoid thinking about anything else. I remembered when we'd sat on the bench, in the gardens of the Champs-Elysées, and he'd photographed his shoes.

And once again, mountain slopes of an eternal whiteness beneath the sun, the narrow streets and deserted squares of the South of France, several photos all with the same caption: *Paris in July*—my birth month, when the city seemed abandoned. But Jansen, in order to fight against the impression of emptiness and neglect, had tried to capture an entirely rural aspect of Paris: curtains of trees, canal, cobblestones in the shade of plane trees, the clock tower of Saint-Germain de Charonne, the steps on Rue des Cascades . . . He was seeking a lost innocence and settings made for enjoyment and ease, but where one could never be happy again.

He thought a photographer was nothing, that he should blend into the surroundings and become invisible, the better to work and capture—as he said—natural light. One shouldn't even hear the click of the Rolleiflex. He would have liked to conceal his camera. The death of his friend Robert Capa could in fact be explained, as he saw it, by this desire, the giddiness of blending into the surroundings once and for all.

Yesterday was Easter Monday. I was walking along the portion of Boulevard Saint-Michel that stretches from the old Luxembourg station to Port-Royal. Strollers were crowded around the entrance gates to the gardens, but where I was walking there was practically no one. One afternoon, on that same stretch of sidewalk, Jansen had pointed out the bookstore at the corner of the boulevard and tiny Rue Royer-Collard. In it, just before the war, he had seen an exhibit of photographs by the painter Wols. He'd gotten to know the artist and admired him as much as he did Capa. He'd gone to visit him in Cassis, where Wols had taken refuge at the start of the Occupation. It was Wols who had taught him to photograph his shoes.

That day, Jansen had drawn my attention to the façade of the Ecole des Mines, an entire section of which, at eye level, was riddled with bullet holes. A plaque, cracked and slightly worn around the edges, noted that a certain Jean Monvallier Boulogne, age twenty, had been killed at that spot on the day Paris was liberated.

I'd remembered that name because of its sonority, which conjured up images of rowing a boat in the Bois de Boulogne with a blonde, a country picnic on the riverbank, a small valley with that same blonde and some friends—all of it cut short one afternoon in August, in front of this wall.

Now, that Monday, to my great surprise, the plaque had disappeared, and I was sorry that Jansen, on the afternoon when we were in that same spot together, hadn't taken a picture of it and the bullet-pocked wall. I would have put it in the index. But now, suddenly, I was no longer sure Jean Monvallier Boulogne had ever existed, and moreover I was no longer sure of anything.

I entered the gardens, slicing through the people massed around the fence. Every bench and every chair was filled and the paths were crowded. Young people were sitting on the terrace rails and the steps leading down to the main fountain, so thick that you couldn't get to that part of the garden. But none of it mattered. I was happy to lose myself in that crowd and—as Jansen would have said—to blend into the surroundings.

Enough space remained—about eight inches—for me to sit at the end of a bench. My neighbors didn't even need to squeeze over. We were beneath chestnut trees that protected us from the sun, right near the white marble statue of Velléda. A woman behind me was chatting with a friend and their words lulled me: something about a certain Suzanne, who had been married to a certain Raymond. Raymond was a friend of Robert, and Robert the brother of one of the women. At first I tried to pay attention to what they were saying and gather some details that could act as reference points, so that the fates of Robert, Suzanne, and Raymond would gradually emerge from obscurity. Who knows? It's possible that, by chance, whose infinite combinations will always remain a mystery, Suzanne, Robert, and Raymond might have crossed paths with Jansen one day in the street.

I was overcome by drowsiness. Words still reached me through a sundrenched fog: Raymond . . . Suzanne . . . Livry-Gargan . . . When you get down to it . . . Eye problems . . . Eze-sur-Mer, near Nice . . . The firehouse on Boulevard Diderot . . . The flow of passersby along the paths compounded this state of half-sleep. I recalled Jansen's reflection, "Don't let it faze you, kid. I've fallen into my share of black holes too . . ." But this time, it wasn't a black hole like the one I'd experienced at nineteen at the Café de la Paix. I was almost relieved at this progressive loss of identity. I could still make out a few words, as the women's voices became softer, more distant. La Ferté-Alais . . . Skirt-chaser . . . Repaid in kind . . . Camper . . . Trip around the world . . .

I was going to disappear in this garden, amid the Easter Monday crowds. I was losing my memory and couldn't understand French anymore, as the words of the women next to me had now become no more than onomatopoeias in my ear. The efforts I'd made for thirty years to have a trade, give my life some coherence, try to speak and write a language as best I could so as to be certain of my nationality—all that tension suddenly released. It was over. I was nothing now. Soon I would slip out of this park toward a metro stop, then a train station and a port. When the gates closed, all that would remain of me would be the raincoat I'd been wearing, rolled into a ball on a bench.

I remember that in the final days before he dropped out of sight, Jansen seemed at once absent and more preoccupied than usual. I'd say something to him and he wouldn't answer. Or else, as if I'd interrupted his train of thought, he'd jump and politely ask me to repeat what I'd just said.

One evening, I had walked with him to his hotel on Boulevard Raspail, for it was less and less often that he slept in the studio. He'd pointed out that the hotel was only a hundred yards away from the one he'd lived in when he first came to Paris and that it had taken him almost thirty years to travel that short distance.

His face darkened and I could sense he wanted to tell me something. Finally he made up his mind to talk, but with such reticence that his statements were muddled, as if he had trouble expressing himself in French. From what I could understand, he had gone to the Belgian and Italian consulates to get a copy of his birth certificate and other documents he needed in anticipation of his departure. There had been some confusion. From Antwerp, his birthplace, they had sent the Italian consulate the records for a different Francis Jansen, and that one was dead.

I suppose he'd called from the studio to get further information about this homonym, since I found the following words on the flyleaf of the notebook in which I'd indexed his photos, scrawled in his near illegible handwriting, in Italian, as if they had been dictated to him: "Jansen Francis, nato a Herenthals in Belgio il 25 aprile 1917. Arrestato a Roma. Detenuto a Roma, Fossoli campo. Deportato da Fossoli il 26 giugno 1944. Deceduto in luogo e data ignoti."

That evening, we had walked by his hotel and continued on toward the Carrefour Montparnasse. He no longer knew which man he was. He told me that after a certain number of years, we accept a truth that we've intuited but kept hidden from ourselves, out of carelessness or cowardice: a brother, a double died in our stead on an unknown date and in an unknown place, and his shadow ends up merging with us.

SUSPENDED SENTENCES

For Dominique

> There is scarce a family that can count four generations but lays a claim to some dormant title or some castle and estate: a claim not prosecutable in any court of law, but flattering to the fancy and a great alleviation of idle hours. A man's claim to his own past is yet less valid.
>
> —Robert Louis Stevenson,
> "A Chapter on Dreams"

It was in the days when theater companies toured not just France, Switzerland, and Belgium, but also North Africa. I was ten years old. My mother had gone on the road for a play, and my brother and I were living with friends of hers, in a small town just outside of Paris.

A two-story house with an ivy-covered façade. One of the windows—the kind they call bow windows—extended from the living room. Behind the house, a terraced garden. Hidden at the back of the first terrace, under a clematis, was the grave of Doctor Guillotin. Had he lived in that house? Was it where he'd perfected his device for severing heads? At the very top of the garden were two apple trees and a pear tree.

Small enamel tags hanging from silver chains around the liquor decanters bore names like Izarra, Sherry, Curaçao. Honeysuckle invaded the sloping roof of the well, in the middle of the courtyard just before the garden. The telephone sat on a pedestal table next to one of the living room windows.

A fence protected the front of the house, which stood back slightly from Rue du Docteur-Dordaine. One day they'd repainted the fence after coating it with red lead. Was it really red lead, that sickly orange coating that remains so vivid in my memory? Rue du Docteur-Dordaine looked like a village street, especially at the far end: a nuns' convent, then a farm where we went to get milk, and beyond that, the chateau. If you walked down the street on the right-hand sidewalk, you went past the post office; across the street, on the left, you could make out behind a fence the nursery of the florist whose son sat next to me in class. A little farther on, on the same side as the post office, the wall of the Jeanne d'Arc school, tucked away behind the leaves of the plane trees.

Opposite our house was a gently sloping avenue. It was bordered on the right by the Protestant temple and by a small wooded area, in the thickets of which we'd found a German soldier's helmet; on the left, by a long, white house with pediments, which had a large garden and a weeping willow. Farther down, adjacent to the garden, was the Robin des Bois inn.

At the bottom of the avenue, and perpendicular to it, was the main road. Toward the right, the perpetually deserted square in front of the train station, where we learned how to ride bikes. In the other direction, you skirted the town park. On the left-hand sidewalk was a kind of concrete mall that housed, all in a row, the news dealer's, the movie theater, and the drugstore. The druggist's son was one of my schoolmates and, one night, his father hanged himself from a rope that he'd attached to the mall balcony. It seems people hang themselves in summer. In the other seasons, they prefer drowning in rivers. That's what the mayor had told the news dealer.

After that, an empty lot where they held the market every Friday. Sometimes the big top of a traveling circus set up there, or the stalls of a fairground.

You then came to the town hall and the grade crossing. After passing over the latter, you followed the high road that went up to the church square and the monument to the dead. For one Christmas Mass, my brother and I had been choirboys in that church.

There were only women in the house where the two of us lived.

Little Hélène was a brunette of about forty, with a wide forehead and prominent cheekbones. Her very short stature made her seem more like us. She had a slight limp from an accident on the job. She had been a circus rider, then an acrobat, and that gave her a certain cachet in our eyes. The circus—as my brother and I had discovered one afternoon at the Médrano—was a world we wanted to join. She told us she'd stopped plying her trade a long time ago and she showed us a photo album with pictures of her in her rider's and acrobat's costumes, and pages from music hall programs that mentioned her name: Hélène Toch. I often asked her to lend me the album so I could look through it in bed, before going to sleep.

They formed a curious trio: she, Annie, and Annie's mother, Mathilde F. Annie had short blond hair, a straight nose, a soft, delicate face, and light-colored eyes. But there was a toughness about her that clashed with the softness of her face, perhaps due to the old brown leather jacket—a man's jacket—that she wore over very tight black trousers during the day. In the evening, she often wore a light blue dress cinched at the waist by a wide black belt, and I liked her better that way.

Annie's mother didn't look anything like her. Was she really her mother? Annie called her Mathilde. Gray hair in a bun. A hard face. Always dressed in dark clothes. I was scared of her. To me she looked old, and yet she really wasn't: Annie was twenty-six at the time and her mother about fifty. I remember the cameos she pinned to her blouse. She had a southern accent that I later heard in natives of

Nîmes. Annie didn't sound like that herself; like my brother and me, she had a Paris accent.

Whenever Mathilde talked to me, she called me "blissful idiot." One morning as I was coming down from my room for breakfast, she'd said as usual:

"Good morning, blissful idiot."

And I'd said:

"Good morning, Madame."

And after all these years, I can still hear her answer in her cutting voice with its Nîmes accent:

"'Madame'? You can call me Mathilde, blissful idiot."

Little Hélène, beneath her kindness, must have been tough as nails.

I learned later that she'd met Annie when the latter was nineteen. She wielded such influence over Annie and her mother, Mathilde F., that the two women had gone off with her, abandoning Mr. F.

One day, no doubt, the circus Little Hélène worked in had stopped in the provincial backwater where Annie and her mother lived. Annie had sat near the orchestra, and the trumpets announced the arrival of Little Hélène, who was riding a black stallion with a silver caparison. Or else I imagine her way up high, on the trapeze, getting ready for the perilous triple flip.

And Annie goes to see her after the show, in the trailer that Little Hélène shares with the snake lady.

A friend of Annie F.'s often came to the house. Her name was Frede. Today, from my adult perspective, she's nothing more than a woman who, in the 1950s, owned a nightclub on Rue Ponthieu. At the time, she seemed to be the same age as Annie, but she was actually a bit older, around thirty-five. A short-haired brunette, with a sylph-like body and pale skin. She wore men's jackets, cinched at the waist, which I took to be riding jackets.

The other day, at a bookstall, I was leafing through an old back issue of *La Semaine à Paris* from July 1939, which had the movie, theater, music hall, and cabaret listings. I was surprised to come across a tiny photo of Frede: when she was twenty, she was already master of ceremonies in a nightclub. I bought this program, the way you buy a piece of evidence, some tangible proof that it wasn't all in your head.

It reads:

THE SILHOUETTE
58, Rue Notre-Dame-de-Lorette
Montmartre, TRI 64-72
FREDE presents
from 10 p.m. til dawn
her all-female Dance-Cabaret
Back from Switzerland
DON MARYO and his famous Orchestra
Guitarist Isidore Langlois
Betty and the Nice Boys

And, fleetingly, I recall the image my brother and I had of Frede whenever we saw her in the garden, as we were returning home from school: a woman who belonged to the world of the circus, like Little Hélène, and whom this world haloed in mystery. We were absolutely certain that Frede operated a circus in Paris, a smaller one than the Médrano, a circus beneath a white canvas big top with red stripes that was called "Carroll's." This name was frequently heard in Annie's and Frede's mouths: Carroll's was a nightclub on Rue de Ponthieu, but I imagined the white-and-red big top and the circus animals, of which Frede, with her svelte silhouette and cinched jackets, was the tamer.

Sometimes on Thursdays, when we didn't have school, she brought her nephew to the house, a boy our age. And the three of us would spend the afternoon playing together. He knew much more than we did about Carroll's. I remember a sibylline statement he'd made to us, which still resonates with me:

"Annie cried all night long at Carroll's . . ."

Perhaps he'd heard that sentence from his aunt, without knowing what it meant. When she didn't bring him, my brother and I would go meet him at the train station, in the early afternoon. We never called him by his name, which we didn't know. We just called him "Frede's nephew."

They hired a girl to come pick me up at school and look after us. She lived in the house, in the room next to ours. She wore her black hair in a very strict bun, and her eyes were of such light green that her gaze seemed transparent. She almost never spoke. Her silence and transparent eyes intimidated my brother and me. For us, Little Hélène, Frede, and even Annie belonged to the world of the circus, but that silent young girl with her black bun and pale eyes was a creature from a fairy tale. We called her Snow White.

I still remember dinners when we were all together in the room that served as dining room, which was separated from the living room by the entrance hall. Snow White was sitting at the end of the table, my brother to her right, and I to her left. Annie was next to me, Little Hélène opposite, and Mathilde at the other end of the table. One evening, because the electricity was out, the room was lit by an oil lamp set on the mantelpiece, which left areas of shadow around us.

The others called her Snow White, like us, and sometimes "my lamb." They used the familiar *tu* with her. And soon a certain intimacy grew among them, since Snow White also addressed them familiarly.

I suppose they had rented the house. Unless Little Hélène owned it, as the village merchants seemed to know her. Or maybe the house belonged to Frede. I remember that Frede received a lot of mail at Rue du Docteur-Dordaine. I was the one who fetched the letters from the box, every morning before school.

Almost every day, Annie went to Paris in her tan Peugeot 4CV. She would come home very late, and sometimes she stayed out until the next day. Often Little Hélène went with her. Mathilde never left the house, except to do the shopping. She'd buy a magazine called *Noir et Blanc*, old copies of which lay around the dining room. I'd leaf through them on Thursday afternoons, when it was raining and we were listening to a children's program on the radio. Mathilde ripped *Noir et Blanc* out of my hands.

"That's not for you, blissful idiot! You're not old enough . . ."

Snow White waited for me when class got out, with my brother, who was still too little to start school. Annie had enrolled me in the Jeanne d'Arc school, at the very end of Rue du Docteur-Dordaine. The principal had asked if she was my mother and she'd said yes.

We were both sitting outside the principal's office. Annie was wearing her old leather jacket and a pair of faded blue denim pants that a friend of hers who sometimes came to the house—Zina Rachevsky—had brought her back from America: blue jeans. You didn't see them very often in France at the time. The principal looked at us suspiciously:

"Your son will have to wear a gray smock in class," she said. "Like all his other little schoolmates."

On the way back, all along Rue du Docteur-Dordaine, Annie walked next to me with her hand on my shoulder.

"I told her I was your mother because it was too complicated to explain the situation. That okay with you, Patoche?"

As for me, I was wondering about that gray smock I'd have to wear, like all my other little schoolmates.

I didn't remain a pupil at the Jeanne d'Arc school for long. The schoolyard was black because it was paved with coal slag. And that black went perfectly with the bark and leaves of the plane trees.

One morning, during recess, the principal came up to me and said:

"I wish to see your mother. Tell her to come this afternoon, as soon as class resumes."

As always, she spoke to me in cutting tones. She didn't like me. What had I ever done to her?

When I left school at lunchtime, Snow White and my brother were waiting.

"*You're* making a face," said Snow White. "Something the matter?"

I asked if Annie was home. My one fear was that she hadn't come back from Paris the night before.

As luck would have it, she had come home, but very late. She was still asleep in her room at the end of the hall, the one whose windows opened onto the garden.

"Go wake her up," said Little Hélène, after I'd related that the school principal wanted to see my mother.

I knocked on the door to her room. She didn't answer. The mysterious sentence we'd heard from Frede's nephew crossed my mind: "Annie cried all night long at Carroll's." Yes, she was still asleep at noon because she'd spent all night crying at Carroll's.

I turned the knob and pushed the door open, slowly. It was light in the room. Annie hadn't drawn the curtains. She was stretched out on the large bed, all the way at the edge, and she could have fallen off at any moment. Why didn't she lie in the middle of the bed? She was sleeping, her arm folded up on her shoulder, as if she were cold, and yet she was fully dressed. She hadn't even removed her shoes or her old leather jacket. I gently shook her shoulder. She opened her eyes and looked at me, knitting her brow:

"Oh . . . It's you, Patoche . . ."

She was pacing back and forth beneath the plane trees in the schoolyard, with the principal of the Jeanne d'Arc school. The principal had told me to wait for them in the yard while they talked. My schoolmates had gone back to class when the bell had rung at five minutes to two, and I watched them, there, behind the panes of glass, sitting at their desks, without me. I tried to hear what the two women were saying, but I didn't dare go any nearer to them. Annie was wearing her old leather jacket over a man's shirt.

And then she walked away from the principal and came up to me. The two of us went out through the little doorway cut into the wall, which led to Rue du Docteur-Dordaine.

"Poor Patoche . . . They've expelled you."

I felt like crying, but when I looked up at her, I saw she was smiling. And that made me feel relieved.

"You're a bad student . . . like me . . ."

Yes, I was relieved that she wouldn't scold me, but all the same I was surprised that this event, which seemed so serious to me, made her smile.

"Don't you fret, old Patoche . . . We'll find you another school."

I don't think I was a worse student than anyone else. The principal of the Jeanne d'Arc school had no doubt gathered information about my family. She must have realized Annie was not my mother. Annie, Little Hélène, Mathilde, and even Snow White: curious family . . . She must have feared I'd set a poor example for my little schoolmates. What could she have had against us? First, Annie's lie. It must have caught the principal's attention right from the get-go: Annie looked younger than her age, and it might have been better if she'd claimed to be my older sister. And then her worn leather jacket and especially those faded blue jeans, which were so unusual at the time . . . Nothing to hold against Mathilde: a typical old woman, with her dark clothes, corsage, cameo, and Nîmes accent. On the other hand, Little Hélène sometimes dressed strangely when she took us to Mass or the village shops: riding breeches with boots, blouses with puffy sleeves drawn tight at the wrists, black ski pants, or even a bolero jacket encrusted with mother-of-pearl . . . You could tell what her former occupation had been. And yet, the news dealer and the baker seemed fond of her, and always addressed her with respect:

"Good afternoon, Mademoiselle Toch . . . Good-bye, Mademoiselle Toch . . . What shall it be for Mademoiselle Toch today . . . ?"

And what could one hold against Snow White? Her silence, black bun, and transparent eyes commanded respect. The principal of the Jeanne d'Arc school surely wondered why that girl came to fetch me after school, instead of my mother; and why I didn't just go home by myself, like my other little friends. She must have thought we were rich.

Who knows? All the principal had to do was lay eyes on Annie for her to distrust us. Even I, one evening, had overheard a few bits of conversation between Little Hélène and Mathilde. Annie hadn't got back from Paris yet in her 4CV and Mathilde seemed anxious.

"I wouldn't put anything past her," Mathilde had said, looking pensive. "You know as well as I do what a hothead she is, Linou."

"She wouldn't do anything really serious," Little Hélène had said.

Mathilde had remained silent a moment, then said:

"You know, Linou, you keep some mighty peculiar company . . ."

Little Hélène's face had grown hard.

"Peculiar? What's that supposed to mean, Thilda?"

She'd spoken in a harsh voice I'd never heard from her before.

"Don't get mad, Linou," Mathilde had said, sounding scared and docile.

This was not the same woman who called me "blissful idiot."

As of that moment, I realized that Annie, during her absences, did not always spend her time crying all night long at Carroll's. She might have been doing something really serious. Later, when I asked what had happened, they told me, "Something very serious," and it was like an echo of the sentence I'd previously heard. But that evening, the expression "hothead" was what worried me. Whenever I looked at Annie's face, all I saw was affection. Could there have been a hothead lurking behind those limpid eyes and that smile?

I was now a pupil at the town public school, a bit farther away than Jeanne d'Arc. You had to follow Rue du Docteur-Dordaine to the end and cross the road that descended toward the town hall and the grade crossing. A large iron double gate led to the recess yard.

Here, too, we wore gray smocks, but the yard wasn't paved with slag. It was just dirt, plain and simple. The teacher liked me and every morning asked me to read a poem to the class. One day, Little Hélène came to fetch me, instead of Snow White. She was wearing her riding breeches, boots, and a jacket that I called her "cowboy jacket." She shook the teacher's hand and told him she was my aunt.

"Your nephew reads poetry very well," the teacher had said.

I always read the same one, the one my brother and I knew by heart:

Oh how many sailors, how many captains . . .

I had some good friends in that class: the son of the florist on Rue du Docteur-Dordaine; the pharmacist's son, and I remember the morning when we learned his father had hanged himself; the son of the baker at the Food Hamlet, whose sister was my age and had blond, curly hair that fell to her ankles.

Often Snow White didn't come to fetch me: she knew I'd come home with the florist's son, whose house was next door to ours. When school got out, on afternoons when we didn't have any homework, a group of us would go to the other end of town, past the chateau and the train station, all the way to the large water mill, on the banks of the Bièvre. It was still operational, and yet it looked dilapidated and abandoned. On Thursdays when Frede's nephew wasn't there, I'd bring my brother. It was an adventure we had to keep secret. We slipped through the gap in the surrounding wall and sat on the ground, side by side. The huge wheel turned round and round. We could hear the rumbling of a motor and the roar of the waterfall. It felt cool here, and it smelled like water and wet grass. The huge wheel gleaming in the half-darkness frightened us a bit, but we couldn't help watching it turn, sitting side by side, arms hugging our knees.

My father would visit between trips to Brazzaville. He didn't drive, and since someone had to bring him from Paris to our town, his friends would pick him up by turns: Annet Badel, Sasha Gordine, Robert Fly, Jacques Boudot-Lamotte, Georges Giorgini, Geza Pellmont, fat Lucien P., who would sit on an armchair in the living room, and each time we were afraid the chair would collapse or split beneath him; Stioppa de D., who wore a monocle and a fur coat, and whose hair was so thick with pomade that it left stains on the couches and walls against which Stioppa leaned his neck.

These visits occurred on Thursdays, and my father would take us out to lunch at the Robin des Bois inn. Annie and Little Hélène were out. Mathilde stayed home. Only Snow White would come to lunch with us. And sometimes Frede's nephew.

My father had been a regular at the Robin des Bois a long time ago. He talked about it during one of our lunches with his friend Geza Pellmont, and I listened in on their conversation.

"You remember?" Pellmont had said. "We used to come here with Eliot Salter . . ."

"The chateau's in ruins," my father had said.

The chateau was at the end of Rue du Docteur-Dordaine, across from the Jeanne d'Arc school. Attached to the half-open gate was a rotting wooden sign, on which one could still read, "Property commandeered by the U.S. Army for Brigadier General Frank Allen." On Thursdays we'd slip between the panels of the gate. The overgrown field of grass came to our waists. At the far end rose a Louis XIII–style chateau, its façade flanked by two detached houses standing forward from it. I later learned that it had been built at the end of the nineteenth century. We flew a kite in the field, a kite made of blue-and-red canvas and shaped like an airplane. We had a hard time getting it to soar very high. Farther on, to the right of the chateau, was a knoll with pine trees, and a stone bench on which Snow White sat. She read *Noir et Blanc* or else did her knitting, while we climbed into the pine branches. But we got dizzy, my brother and I, and only Frede's nephew made it to the top.

Toward midafternoon, we followed the path leading away from the knoll and, along with Snow White, we penetrated into the forest. We walked all the way to the Food Hamlet. In autumn we'd gather chestnuts. The baker at the Hamlet was my schoolmate's dad, and every time we went into his shop my friend's sister was there, and I admired her wavy blond hair that fell to her ankles. And then we went back by the same path. In the twilight, the façade and two forward-projecting outbuildings of the chateau looked sinister and made our hearts pound, my brother's and mine.

"Shall we go see the chateau?"

From then on, these were the words my father spoke at the end of every lunch. And just like the other Thursdays, we followed Rue du Docteur-Dordaine and slipped through the half-open gate into the field. Except that, on those days, my father and one of his friends — Badel, Gordine, Stioppa, or Robert Fly — came with us.

Snow White went to sit on the bench at the base of the pines, in her usual spot. My father approached the chateau, contemplating the façade and the tall, boarded-up windows. He pushed open the main door and we walked into a grand entrance hall, whose tiling was buried under rubble and dead leaves. At the back of the hall was an elevator cage.

"I used to know the owner of this chateau," said my father.

He could see my brother and I were curious. So he told us the story of Eliot Salter, the marquis de Caussade, who, at the age of twenty, during the First World War, had been a flying ace. Then he'd married an Argentinian woman and become the king of Armagnac. Armagnac, said my father, was a liqueur that Salter, the marquis de Caussade, made and sold in very handsome bottles by the truckload. I helped him unload all those trucks, said my father. We counted the cases, one by one. He had bought this chateau. He had disappeared at the end of the last war with his wife, but he wasn't dead and someday he'd be back.

Gingerly my father peeled off a small notice affixed to the inside of the front door and gave it to me. Even today, without the slightest hesitation, I can still recite what was written on it:

Seizure of illegal gains
Tuesday, July 23, at 2:00 p.m.
At the Food Hamlet
Magnificent property
including chateau and 750 acres of forestland

"Keep an eye on this place, boys," said my father. "The marquis
will be back, and sooner than you think . . ."

And before getting into the car of whatever friend was driving
him that day, he bid us good-bye with a distracted hand, which we
could still see waving limply through the window as the car headed
off to Paris.

We had decided, my brother and I, to visit the chateau at night. We had to wait until everyone in the house was asleep. Mathilde's room took up the ground floor of a tiny cottage at the back of the court-yard: no danger of her hearing us. Little Hélène's room was upstairs in the house, at the other end of the hall, and Snow White's was next to ours. The hall floor creaked a bit, but once we made it to the foot of the stairs we'd have nothing to fear and it would be clear sailing. We would pick a night when Annie wasn't home, as she went to bed very late—a night when she was crying at Carroll's.

We'd taken the flashlight from the kitchen cupboard, a silvery metal flashlight that produced a yellowish beam. And we got dressed. We left on our pajama tops under our sweaters. To keep awake, we talked about Eliot Salter, the marquis de Caussade. Taking turns, we came up with the wildest tales about him. On the nights when he visited the chateau, according to my brother, he arrived at the local station on the last train from Paris, the eleven-thirty-three, whose rhythmic rumbling we could hear from our bedroom window. He liked to avoid drawing attention to himself and so didn't park his car in front of the chateau gate, which would have aroused suspicion. Instead, it was on foot, like a simple pedestrian, that he went to his property for the night.

We were both convinced of the same thing: on those nights, Eliot Salter, the marquis de Caussade, stayed in the great hall of the chateau. Before his arrival, someone had swept up the dead leaves and rubble, and afterward they would put it all back to cover every trace of his pas-sage. And the person who made these preparations for his master's visit was the gamekeeper. He lived in the forest, between the Food Hamlet and the edge of the Villacoublay airfield. We often met him during our walks with Snow White. We had asked the baker's son for the name of this faithful servant who hid his secret so well: Grosclaude.

It was no coincidence that Grosclaude lived there. We had discovered, in that area of the forest that bordered the airfield, an abandoned landing strip with a large hangar. The marquis used that landing strip at night, to head off in an airplane toward some faraway destination—an island in the South Seas. After a while, he would return from there. And on those nights, Grosclaude would set out small light signals so the marquis could land more easily.

The marquis was sitting in a velvet armchair in front of the massive fireplace where Grosclaude had lit a fire. Behind him, the table was set: silver candelabras, lace, and crystal. We entered the great hall, my brother and I. The only light was from the fire in the fireplace and the flame of the candles. Grosclaude saw us first and came charging up to us, with his boots and riding breeches.

"What do you think you're doing here?"

His voice was threatening. He'd surely give us both a couple of slaps and throw us out. It would be better if, when we entered the hall, we went straight up to the marquis de Caussade and talked to him directly. And we tried to plan in advance what we would say.

"We've come to see you because you're a friend of my father's."

I would be the one to speak that first sentence. After that, in turn, we'd say:

"Good evening, my Lord."

And I would add:

"We know that you're the king of Armagnac."

Still, there was one detail that worried me: the moment when the marquis Eliot Salter de Caussade turned his face toward us. My father had told us that his face had been burned during an aerial battle in the First World War, and that he concealed this burn by covering his skin with ochre-colored makeup. In that entrance hall, in the light of the candles and the wood fire, that face must have been terrifying. But at least I would finally see what I tried to see behind Annie's smile and bright eyes: a hothead.

We had crept down the stairs on tiptoe, our shoes in our hands. The kitchen clock said eleven-twenty-five. We had gently closed the front door to the house and the small metal gate that opened onto Rue du Docteur-Dordaine. Sitting on the curb, we laced up our shoes. The rumble of the train was approaching. It would be in the station in a few minutes and would leave only a single passenger on the platform: Eliot Salter, the marquis de Caussade and the king of Armagnac.

We chose nights when the sky was clear, when the stars shone around a sliver of moon. Our shoes tied, the flashlight hidden between my sweater and my pajama top, we now had to walk to the chateau. The empty street in the moonlight, the silence, and the feeling that came over us of having left home for good gradually made us slow our steps. After about fifty yards, we turned back.

Now we unlaced our shoes and gently closed the front door to the house. The alarm clock in the kitchen said twenty minutes to midnight. I put the flashlight back in the cupboard and we tiptoed back up the stairs.

Huddled in our twin beds, we felt a certain relief. We spoke in low whispers about the marquis, and each of us came up with a new detail. It was past midnight, and over there, in the great hall, Grosclaude was serving him his supper. The next time, before turning back, we'd go a bit farther down Rue du Docteur-Dordaine than we had this time. We'd go as far as the convent. And the next time after that, even farther, up to the farm and the barbershop. And the time after that, farther still. A new milestone every night. Then there would only be a few dozen yards to go before we reached the chateau fence. The next time . . . We ended up falling asleep.

I had noticed that Annie and Little Hélène occasionally received visits at the house from people as mysterious and worthy of interest as Eliot Salter, the marquis de Caussade.

Was it Annie who kept up the friendships? Or Little Hélène? Both, I think. For her part, Mathilde maintained a certain reserve in their presence, and often she went to her room. Perhaps those people intimidated her, or maybe she just didn't like them.

I'm trying today to count all the faces I saw on the front porch or in the living room — without being able to identify most of them. No matter. If I could put names to those ten or so faces parading through my memory, it would prove embarrassing for some people who are still alive. They'd remember that they used to keep bad company.

The ones whose images remain the clearest are Roger Vincent, Jean D., and Andrée K., who they said was "the wife of a big-shot doctor." They came to the house two or three times a week. They went to have lunch at the Robin des Bois inn with Annie and Little Hélène, and afterward they'd sit around a while longer in the living room. Or else they stayed for dinner at the house.

Sometimes Jean D. came alone. Annie would bring him from Paris in her 4CV. He was the one who seemed closest to Annie and who had probably introduced her to the two others. Jean D. and Annie were the same age. When Jean D. came to visit with Roger Vincent, it was always in Roger Vincent's American convertible. Sometimes Andrée K. came with them, and she would sit in the front seat of the American car, next to Roger Vincent; Jean D. was in back. Roger Vincent must have been around forty-five at the time, and Andrée K. thirty-five.

I remember the first time we saw Roger Vincent's American car parked in front of the house. It was the end of the morning, after class. I hadn't yet been expelled from the Jeanne d'Arc school. From a distance, that huge convertible, with its tan body and red leather seats gleaming in the sun, had surprised my brother and me as much as if we'd turned a corner in the road and suddenly found ourselves face to face with the marquis de Caussade. Moreover, we'd had the same thought at the same moment, as we later confided to each other: the car belonged to the marquis de Caussade, who was back in the village after all his adventures and had been invited over by my father.

I said to Snow White:

"Whose car is that?"

"A friend of your godmother's."

She always called Annie my "godmother," and it was in fact the case that we'd been baptized one year earlier at the church of Saint-Martin de Biarritz and that my mother had asked Annie to act as my godmother.

When we went inside the house, the living room door was open and Roger Vincent was sitting on the couch, next to the bow window.

"Come say hello," said Little Hélène.

She had just poured out three glasses and was stopping up one of the liquor decanters with the enamel tags. Annie was on the telephone.

Roger Vincent stood up. He seemed very tall. He was wearing a glen plaid suit. His hair was white, well groomed, and brushed back, but he didn't seem old. He leaned toward us and smiled.

"Hello, children . . ."

He shook our hands in turn. I had put down my schoolbag to shake his. I was wearing my gray smock.

"Are you just getting home from school?"

"Yes," I said.

"School going well?"

"Yes."

Annie had hung up the phone and joined us; Little Hélène set the liquor tray on the coffee table in front of the couch. She handed Roger Vincent a glass.

"Patoche and his brother live here," Annie said.

"Well, then, to the health of Patoche and his brother," said Roger Vincent, raising his glass with a wide smile.

In my memory, that smile remains Roger Vincent's main attribute: it was always playing about his lips. Roger Vincent bathed in that smile, which was distant and dreamy rather than jovial, and which enveloped him like a very light mist. There was something muffled about that smile, as about his voice and bearing. Roger Vincent never made any noise. You never heard him coming, and when you turned around, there he was behind you. From the window of our room, we sometimes saw him arrive at the wheel of his American car. It stopped in front of the house like a speedboat with its motor cut off, carried in by the tide to berth silently on the shore. Roger Vincent stepped out of the car, his movements slow, his smile on his lips. He never slammed the door, but rather closed it gently.

That day, they were still in the living room when we finished our lunch with Snow White in the kitchen. Mathilde was tending the rose bush she had planted on the first terrace of the garden, near the grave of Doctor Guillotin.

I was holding my satchel, and Snow White was going to take me back to the Jeanne d'Arc school for afternoon classes, when Annie, who had appeared in the doorway to the living room, said to me:

"Study well, Patoche . . ."

Behind her, I saw Little Hélène and Roger Vincent smiling his immutable smile. No doubt they were about to leave the house to go have lunch at the Robin des Bois inn.

"Are you walking to school?" asked Roger Vincent.

"Yes."

Even when he talked, he smiled.

"I can take you in the car, if you like . . ."

"Did you see Roger Vincent's car?" Annie asked me.

"Yes."

She always called him "Roger Vincent," with respectful affection, as if his first and last names were inseparable. I sometimes heard her on the telephone: "Hello, Roger Vincent . . . How are you, Roger Vincent . . ." She used the formal *vous*. She and Jean D. had great admiration for him. Jean D. called him "Roger Vincent" as well. When Annie and Jean D. talked about him, they seemed to be telling "Roger Vincent stories," as if they were recounting ancient legends. Andrée K., "the wife of the big-shot doctor," called him just Roger, and she said *tu*.

"Would you like it if I took you to school in my car?" asked Roger Vincent.

He had guessed what we wanted, my brother and I. We both climbed into the front seat next to him.

He backed majestically up the gentle slope of the avenue, and the car followed Rue du Docteur-Dordaine.

We glided on slack water. I couldn't hear the sound of the motor. It was the first time my brother and I had ridden in a convertible. And that car was so big that it covered the entire width of the street.

"Here's my school . . ."

He stopped the car and, stretching out his arm, opened the passenger door so that I could get out.

"Good luck, Patoche."

I was proud to hear him call me Patoche, as if he'd known me for a long time. My brother was now all alone next to him, and he looked even smaller on that huge red leather seat. I turned around before going into the courtyard of the Jeanne d'Arc school. Roger Vincent waved at me. He was smiling.

Jean D. didn't have an American convertible, but he had a fat wristwatch on whose face we could read the seconds, minutes, hours, days, months, and years. He explained the complicated mechanism of that watch with its many buttons. He was much more at ease with us than Roger Vincent. And younger.

He wore a suede windbreaker, sporty turtleneck sweaters, and shoes with crepe soles. He, too, was tall and thin. Dark hair and a face with regular features. When his brown eyes rested on us, they were lit by a mix of mischief and sadness. His eyes were always widening, as if everything astonished him. I envied him his haircut: a long brush cut, whereas in my case, every two weeks the barber gave me a crew cut so short that the hairs pinched when I ran my hand over my scalp and above my ears. But there was nothing I could say. The barber simply picked up his clippers without asking my opinion.

Jean D. came to the house more often than the others. Annie always brought him in her 4CV. He had lunch with us and always sat next to Annie, at the large dining room table. Mathilde called him "my little Jean," and she didn't show the same reserve with him as she did with the other visitors. He called Little Hélène "Linou"—the same as Mathilde did. He always said, "How's it going, Linou?"—and he called me "Patoche," like Annie.

He lent my brother and me his watch. We were able to wear it, taking turns, for a whole week. The leather strap was too big, so he made another hole in it to keep it tight around our wrists. I wore that watch to the Jeanne d'Arc school and showed it off to the schoolmates huddled around me in the playground that day. Maybe the principal noticed that huge watch on my wrist, and saw me from her window getting out of Roger Vincent's American car . . . Then she thought that was quite enough of that and that my place was not at the Jeanne d'Arc school.

"What sort of books do you read?" Jean D. asked me one day.

They were all having coffee in the living room after lunch: Annie, Mathilde, Little Hélène, and Snow White. It was a Thursday. We were waiting for Frede, who was supposed to arrive with her nephew. We had decided, my brother and I, to venture into the great hall of the chateau that afternoon, as we'd already done with my father. The presence of Frede's nephew at our sides would bolster our courage.

"Patoche reads a ton," answered Annie. "Isn't that so, Snow White?"

"He reads way too much for his age," said Snow White.

My brother and I had dipped a lump of sugar into Annie's coffee cup and crunched it, as our ceremony required. Afterward, when they'd finished their coffee, Mathilde would read their future in the empty cups — "in the dregs," as she said.

"So what do you read?" asked Jean D.

I told him adventure stories: Jules Verne, *The Last of the Mohicans* . . . but I preferred *The Three Musketeers* because of the fleur de lys on Milady's shoulder.

"You should read pulps," said Jean D.

"Jean, you're crazy," said Annie, laughing. "Patoche is way too young for pulps . . ."

"He's got plenty of time ahead of him to read pulps," said Little Hélène.

Apparently, neither Mathilde nor Snow White knew what "pulps" were. They kept silent.

A few days later, he returned to the house in Annie's 4CV. It was raining that late afternoon, and Jean D. was wearing a fur-lined coat called a "Canadienne." My brother and I were listening to the radio, both seated at the dining room table, and when we saw him come in with Annie, we got up to greet him.

"Here," said Jean D., "I brought you a pulp . . ."

He took a black-and-yellow-covered book from the pocket of his jacket and handed it to me.

"Pay no attention, Patoche," said Annie. "He's just joking. That's not a book for you . . ."

Jean D. looked at me with his slightly widened eyes, his sad, tender gaze. At certain moments, I had the sense that he was a child, like us. Annie often spoke to him in the same tone she used with us.

"No, seriously . . ." said Jean D. "I'm sure you'll like this book."

I took it so as not to hurt his feelings. Still today, whenever I come across one of the black-and-yellow covers of the Série Noire, a deep, slightly drawling voice echoes in my head, the voice of Jean D., who that evening repeated to me and my brother the title written on the book he'd given us: *Don't Touch the Loot.*

Was it the same day? It was raining. We had accompanied Snow White to the news dealer's because she wanted to buy some stationery. When we left the house, Annie and Jean D. were both sitting in the 4CV, parked in front of the door. They were talking and were so absorbed in their conversation that they didn't see us, even though I waved at them. Jean D. had pulled the collar of his Canadienne up around his neck. When we returned, they were still in the 4CV. I leaned toward them, but they didn't even look. They were talking and they both had serious faces.

Little Hélène was playing solitaire on the dining room table and listening to the radio. Mathilde must have been in her bedroom. My brother and I went up to ours. Through the window, I watched the 4CV in the rain. They stayed in it, talking, all the way to dinnertime. What secrets could they have been sharing?

Roger Vincent and Jean D. often came for dinner at the house, along with Andrée K. Other guests arrived after dinner. On those evenings, they all stayed in the living room until very late. From our bedroom we could hear shouts and bursts of laughter. And the phone ringing. And the doorbell. We ate dinner at seven-thirty in the kitchen, with Snow White. The dining room table was already set for Roger Vincent, Jean D., Andrée K., Annie, Mathilde, and Little Hélène. Little Hélène cooked for them, and they all said she was "a real cordon bleu."

Before going up to bed, we went into the living room to say good night. We were in our pajamas and bathrobes—two plaid flannel bathrobes that Annie had given us as presents.

The others would join them later in the evening. I couldn't help watching them, through the slats of the blinds in our room, once Snow White had turned out the lights and wished us good night. They came, one by one, and rang at the door. I could easily see their faces under the bright light of the bulb above the porch. Some of them have been engraved indelibly in my memory. And I'm amazed the police never questioned me: children see things, after all. They also hear things.

"You have very handsome bathrobes," said Roger Vincent.

And he smiled.

We first shook Andrée K.'s hand, who always sat on the chair with the flowered upholstery next to the telephone. People called her while she was at the house. Little Hélène, who usually picked up, would say:

"Andrée, it's for you . . ."

Andrée K. stretched out her arm to us nonchalantly. She smiled, too, but her smile didn't last as long as Roger Vincent's.

"Good night, children."

She had freckles on her face, prominent cheekbones, green eyes, and light brown hair cut in bangs. She smoked a lot.

We shook Roger Vincent's hand, who was always smiling. Then Jean D.'s. We kissed Annie and Little Hélène good night. Before leaving the living room with Snow White, Roger Vincent complimented us again on the elegance of our bathrobes.

We were at the foot of the stairs when Jean D. stuck his head through the half-open door to the living room.

"Sleep tight."

He looked at us with his tender, slightly widened eyes. He gave us a wink and said in a lower voice, as if it were our secret:

"Don't touch the loot."

One Thursday, Snow White took a day off. She had gone to visit family in Paris and had left with Annie and Mathilde after lunch, in the 4CV. We stayed home in the care of Little Hélène. We were playing in the garden at setting up a canvas tent Annie had given me for my last birthday. Around midafternoon, Roger Vincent came by, alone. He and Little Hélène talked together in the courtyard of the house, but I couldn't hear what they were saying. Little Hélène told us she had to run an errand in Versailles and asked us to come with them.

We were thrilled to ride in Roger Vincent's American car again. It was April, during Easter vacation. Little Hélène sat in front. She was wearing her riding breeches and her cowboy jacket. We were sitting on the huge back seat, my brother and I, and our feet didn't reach the floor of the car.

Roger Vincent drove slowly. He looked back toward us, with his smile:

"Would you like me to turn on the radio?"

The radio? So you could listen to the radio in this car? He pushed an ivory button on the dashboard, and instantly we heard music.

"Should I turn it up or down, boys?" he asked us.

We didn't dare answer. We listened to the music coming from the dashboard. And then a woman started singing in a raspy voice.

"That's Edith singing, boys," said Roger Vincent. "She's a friend..."

He asked Little Hélène:

"Do you still see Edith?"

"Now and then," said Little Hélène.

We drove down a large avenue and arrived in Versailles. The car stopped at a red light, and we admired, on a lawn to our left, a clock whose numbers were made of flowerbeds.

"The next time," Little Hélène said to us, "I'll take you to see the palace."

She asked Roger Vincent to stop at a store where they sold used furniture.

"Boys, you stay here in the car," said Roger Vincent. "Watch the car for me . . ."

We were proud to be entrusted with such an important mission and we watched the comings and goings of the passers-by like hawks. Behind the window of the store, Roger Vincent and Little Hélène were talking with a dark-haired man wearing a raincoat and a mustache. They spoke for a very long time. They had forgotten about us.

They came out of the store. Roger Vincent was holding a leather suitcase that he stashed in the trunk. He got back behind the wheel, with Little Hélène next to him. He turned back toward me:

"Anything to report?"

"No . . . Nothing . . ." I said.

"So much the better," said Roger Vincent.

On the way back, in Versailles, we followed an avenue at the end of which rose a brick church. Several fairground stalls occupied the median strip, around a glittering bumper car track. Roger Vincent parked along the curb.

"Shall we take them for a ride in the bumper cars?" he asked Little Hélène.

The four of us waited at the side of the track. Music blared very loud through speakers. Only three cars were being used by customers, two of which chased the third and rammed it at the same time, on either side, producing screams and shouts of laughter. The trolley poles left trails of sparks along the ceiling of the track. But what captivated me more than anything was the color of the cars: turquoise,

pale green, yellow, purple, bright red, mauve, pink, midnight blue . . .
They stopped moving and their occupants left the track. My brother
climbed into a yellow car with Roger Vincent, and I, with Little
Hélène, into a turquoise one.

We were the only ones on the track, and we didn't ram each other.
Roger Vincent and Little Hélène drove. We circled the track, and
Little Hélène and I followed Roger Vincent and my brother's car. We
zigzagged among the other cars, empty and motionless. The music
played less loudly, and the man who had sold us our tickets looked
forlorn, standing at the side of the track as if we were the last customers ever.

It was nearly dark. We stopped at the edge of the track. I looked one
more time at all those cars with their bright colors. We talked about
it, my brother and I, in our room after lights out. We had decided to
build a track in the courtyard the next day, with old planks from the
storage shed. Naturally, it wouldn't be easy to get hold of a bumper
car, but maybe you could find old ones that didn't work. It was mainly
the color that interested us: I couldn't decide between mauve and turquoise; my brother had a predilection for very pale green.

The air was warm and Roger Vincent hadn't put down the top of
his convertible. He was talking with Little Hélène, and I was thinking too much about those bumper cars we'd just discovered to listen
to their grown-up conversation. We drove past the airfield and would
soon turn left onto the road that went up to the village. They raised
their voices. They weren't arguing, just talking about Andrée K.

"Sure she was," said Roger Vincent. "Andrée was part of the Rue
Lauriston gang . . ."

"Andrée was part of the Rue Lauriston gang." That sentence had
struck me. In school, we, too, had a gang: the florist's son, the barber's son, and two or three others I don't remember, who all lived on
the same street. They called us "the Rue du Docteur-Dordaine gang."
Andrée K. had been part of a gang, like us, but on a different street.

That woman who so intimidated my brother and me, with her bangs, her freckles, her green eyes, her cigarettes and mysterious phone calls, now suddenly seemed more like us. Roger Vincent and Little Hélène also seemed to be very familiar with that "Rue Lauriston gang." Subsequently, I again overheard the name in their conversation and I became used to the sound of it. A few years later, I heard it in the mouth of my father, but I didn't know that "the Rue Lauriston gang" would haunt me for such a long time.

When we arrived back on Rue du Docteur-Dordaine, Annie's 4CV was there. Behind it was a huge motorcycle. In the vestibule, Jean D. told us the motorcycle was his and that he'd come to the house on it all the way from Paris. He hadn't removed his Canadienne. He promised to take us for a ride on the motorcycle, by turns, but tonight it was too late. Snow White would be back the next morning. Mathilde had already gone to bed, and Annie asked us to go up to our room for a bit because they needed to talk. Roger Vincent went into the living room, leather suitcase in hand. Little Hélène, Annie, and Jean D. followed him in, and they closed the door behind them. I had watched them from the top of the stairs. What could they be saying to each other, there in the living room? I heard the telephone ring.

After a while, Annie called us. We all ate dinner together at the dining room table: Annie, Little Hélène, Jean D., Roger Vincent, and the two of us. That evening, at dinner, we were not wearing our bathrobes, as usual, but rather our daytime clothes. Little Hélène did the cooking because she was a real cordon bleu.

We lived on Rue du Docteur-Dordaine for much more than a year. The seasons follow one another in my memory. In winter, at midnight Mass, we were choirboys in the village church. Annie, Little Hélène, and Mathilde attended Mass. Snow White spent Christmas with her family. When we got back, Roger Vincent was at the house, and he told us someone was waiting in the living room. My brother and I went in and found Santa Claus, sitting on the chair with the flowered upholstery next to the telephone. He didn't speak. He handed each of us, in silence, presents covered in silver paper. But we didn't have a chance to unwrap them. He stood up and motioned for us to follow. He and Roger Vincent led us to the glass-paneled door that looked out on the courtyard. On the wooden planks we had laid end to end, there was a bumper car colored pale green — the way my brother liked them. Then we had dinner together. Jean D. showed up to join us. He had the same height and movements as Santa Claus. And the same watch.

Snow on the playground at school. And freezing rains in March. I had discovered that it rained practically every other day and I could predict the weather. I was always right. For the first time in our lives, we went to the movies. With Snow White. It was a Laurel and Hardy film. The apple trees in the garden flowered anew. Once more, I accompanied the Rue du Docteur-Dordaine gang to the mill, whose large wheel was turning again. We began flying kites again, in front of the chateau. We were no longer afraid, my brother and I, of going into the great hall and walking among the rubble and dead leaves. We sat down at the far end, in the elevator, an elevator with two screen doors, made of light paneled wood and with a red leather bench. It had no ceiling and daylight fell from the top of the shaft, through the still intact skylight. We pushed the buttons and pretended to go up to the various floors, where the marquis Eliot Salter de Caussade might have been expecting us.

But he wasn't seen in town that year. It was very hot. Flies stuck to the flypaper stretched on the wall of the kitchen. We planned a picnic in the forest with Snow White and Frede's nephew. What my brother and I liked best was making the bumper car glide over the old planks — a bumper car that we later learned Little Hélène had found through a friend who worked in a fairground.

On Bastille Day, Roger Vincent took us out to dinner at the Robin des Bois inn. He had come from Paris with Jean D. and Andrée K. We sat at a table in the garden of the inn, a garden decorated with groves and statues. Everyone was there: Annie, Little Hélène, Snow White, and even Mathilde. Annie was wearing her light blue dress and wide black belt that hugged her waist very tight. I was sitting next to Andrée K. and I wanted to ask her about the gang she'd been in, the one on Rue Lauriston, but I didn't dare.

And autumn . . . We went with Snow White to gather chestnuts in the forest. We hadn't heard from our parents. The last postcard from our mother had been a bird's-eye view of the city of Tunis. Our father had written us from Brazzaville. Then from Bangui. And after that, nothing. It was the start of the school season. The teacher, after gym, made us rake up the dead leaves on the playground. In the courtyard of the house we let them fall without raking them up, and they took on a rust-red color that clashed with the light green of the bumper car. The latter seemed stuck for all eternity in the middle of a track of dead leaves. We sat in the bumper car, my brother and I, and I leaned on the steering wheel. Tomorrow we would invent a system to make it glide. Tomorrow . . . Always tomorrow, like those nighttime visits to the marquis de Caussade's chateau that we kept postponing.

There was another power outage, and we lit the house with an oil lamp at dinnertime. On Saturday evening, Mathilde and Snow White lit a fire in the dining room fireplace and let us listen to the radio. Sometimes we heard Edith, who was friends with Roger Vincent and Little Hélène. At night, before falling asleep, I leafed through Little Hélène's photo album, where there were pictures of her, her and her work colleagues. Two particularly impressed me: the American Chester Kingston, whose limbs were as supple as rubber and who could dislocate himself so well that they called him the "puzzle man." And Alfredo Codona, the trapeze artist Little Hélène told us about so often and who had taught her the trade. That world of circuses and music halls was the only one my brother and I wanted to live in, perhaps because our mother used to take us with her, when we were little, into the wings and dressing rooms of the theaters.

The others still came to the house. Roger Vincent, Jean D., Andrée K. . . . And the ones who rang at the door after dark, who I spied on through the slats of the blinds, their faces lit by the bulb above the front door porch. Voices, laughter, and telephone rings. And Annie and Jean D., in the 4CV, in the rain.

I never saw them in the years that followed, except, once, for Jean D. I was twenty years old. I had a room on Rue Coustou, near Place Blanche. I was trying to write my first book. A friend had invited me out to a neighborhood restaurant. When I went to join him, he was with two other guests: Jean D. and a girl who was with him.

Jean D. had hardly aged. A few gray hairs on his temples, but he still had his long brush cut. Tiny wrinkles around the eyes. He wasn't wearing a Canadienne this time, but rather a very elegant gray suit. It occurred to me that we were no longer the same, he and I. Throughout the entire meal, we never once alluded to the old days. He asked what I was doing in life. He used the familiar *tu* and called me Patrick. He had surely explained to the two others that he'd known me for a long time.

As for me, I knew a little more about him than when I was a child. That year, the kidnapping of a Moroccan politician had been front-page news. One of the protagonists in the affair had died under mysterious circumstances, on Rue des Renaudes, just as the police broke down his door. Jean D. was a friend of that person and the last one to see him alive. He had given testimony that had been reported in the papers. But the articles also contained other details: Jean D. had once served seven years in prison. They didn't say why, but, judging from the dates, his troubles had begun around the time we lived on Rue du Docteur-Dordaine.

We didn't say a word about those articles. I simply asked him if he lived in Paris.

"I have an office on Faubourg Saint-Honoré. You'll have to come by . . ."

After dinner, my friend disappeared. I found myself alone with Jean D. and the girl who was with him, a brunette who must have been a dozen years younger than he.

"Can I drop you somewhere?"

He opened the door of a Jaguar parked in front of the restaurant. I had learned from the newspaper accounts that in certain circles they called him "the Tall Man with the Jaguar." Since the start of dinner, I'd been looking for a way to ask him about a past that still remained a mystery.

"Is this car the reason they call you 'the Tall Man with the Jaguar'?" I asked.

But he merely shrugged and didn't answer.

He wanted to see my room on Rue Coustou. He and the girl, behind me, climbed the narrow staircase whose worn red carpet gave off a funny odor. They came into the room and the girl took the one chair—a wicker armchair. Jean D. remained standing.

It was strange to see him in that room, in his elegant gray suit and dark silk tie. The girl looked around her and didn't seem very enthusiastic about the décor.

"So, you're a writer? How's it working out?"

He leaned over the bridge table and looked at the sheets of paper that I labored to fill, day after day.

"You write with a Bic?"

He smiled.

"Does the place have heat?"

"No."

"But you're getting by?"

What could I tell him? That I didn't know how I was going to find five hundred francs to pay the rent this month? Of course we'd known each other a long time, but that was no reason to unburden myself on him.

"I'm getting by," I said.

"Doesn't seem like it."

For a moment, we faced each other in the window frame. Even though they called him "the Tall Man with the Jaguar," I was now a little taller than he was. He covered me with a look that was affectionate and naïve, the same as in the days of Rue du Docteur-Dordaine. He rolled his tongue between his lips, and I remember that he'd done that at the house, too, when he was thinking. That way of rolling his tongue between his lips and being lost in thought is something I later discovered in someone else—the writer Emmanuel Berl—and it moved me.

He kept silent. So did I. His girlfriend was still sitting in the wicker chair and leafing through a magazine that she'd grabbed off the bed. All things considered, it was better that the girl was there, otherwise we would have started talking, Jean D. and I. It hadn't been easy: I could read it in his eyes. At the first words, we would have collapsed like those puppets in shooting galleries when the pellet hits the mark. Annie, Little Hélène, and Roger Vincent had certainly wound up in jail. I had lost my brother. The thread had snapped—a gossamer strand. There was nothing left of all that . . .

He turned to his girlfriend and said:

"There's a nice view from here . . . It's just like the Côte d'Azur."

The window looked out on narrow Rue Puget, where no one ever walked. A shabby bar on the corner, a former Coal and Spirits shop in front of which a solitary streetwalker stood waiting. Always the same. And for nothing.

"Nice view, eh?"

Jean D. inspected the room, the bed, the bridge table at which I wrote every day. I saw him from the back. His friend leaned her forehead against the window and contemplated Rue Puget below.

They left, wishing me good luck. A few moments later, I discovered on the bridge table four five hundred–franc bills, neatly folded. I tried to find the address of his office on Faubourg Saint-Honoré. In vain. And I never again saw the Tall Man with the Jaguar.

On Thursdays and Saturdays when Snow White wasn't there, Annie would take my brother and me to Paris in her 4CV. She always followed the same route and, with some effort of memory, I was able to reconstruct it. We took the western highway and drove through the Saint-Cloud tunnel. We crossed a bridge over the Seine, then went along the river through Boulogne and Neuilly. I remember large houses near the banks, protected by fences and foliage. Also barges and floating houses that one reached via wooden stairs: at the foot of those stairs were mailboxes, each with a name on it.

"I'm going to buy a barge here and we'll all live on it," said Annie.

We arrived at the Porte Maillot. I was able to locate that stop in our itinerary because of the little train in the Jardin d'Acclimatation. Annie had taken us on it one afternoon. And we reached the end-point of our journey, in that zone where Neuilly, Levallois, and Paris all blended together.

It was a street lined with trees, their leaves forming a vault. No dwellings, only warehouses and garages. We stopped in front of the largest and newest garage, with a tan pedimented façade.

Inside, a room was blocked off by glass-paneled walls. A man was waiting for us, with curly blond hair, sitting on a leather chair at a metal desk. He was Annie's age. They spoke familiarly. He was dressed, like Jean D., in a plaid shirt, a suede windbreaker, a Cana-dienne in winter, and crepe-soled shoes. Privately, my brother and I used to call him "Buck Danny," because I thought he looked like a character in an illustrated children's book I was reading at the time.

What could Annie and Buck Danny have had to talk about? What could they have been up to when the office door was locked from the inside and an orange canvas shade came down over the windows? My brother and I would wander around the garage, which was even more mysterious than the great hall of the chateau abandoned by Eliot Salter, the marquis de Caussade. One by one we pondered the cars that were missing a fender, a hood, a rubber tire on a wheel. A man in overalls was lying under a convertible and repairing something with a monkey wrench; another, hose in hand, was filling the gas tank of a truck that had come to a halt with a terrible snorting of its engine. One day, we recognized Roger Vincent's American car, its hood open, and we concluded that Buck Danny and Roger Vincent were friends.

Sometimes we'd go to meet Buck Danny at his home, in an apartment building on the boulevard, which I now think was Boulevard Berthier. We'd wait for Annie on the sidewalk. She came out with Buck Danny. We'd leave the 4CV parked in front of the building and walk, the four of us, to the garage, down narrow streets lined with trees and warehouses.

It was cool in the garage, and the smell of gasoline was stronger than the smell of cut grass or water when we sat by the mill wheel. The same kind of shadow floated over certain corners, where neglected cars slumbered. Their bodies shone dimly in that half-light, and I couldn't stop looking at a metal plaque affixed to the wall, a yellow plaque on which I read a seven-letter name in black letters, the design and sound of which still move me even today: CASTROL.

One Thursday she took me alone in her 4CV. My brother had gone shopping with Little Hélène in Versailles. We parked in front of the apartment building where Buck Danny lived. But this time, she came back out without him.

At the garage, he wasn't in his office. We got back into the 4CV and drove through the narrow streets of the quarter. We lost our way. We turned round and round in those streets that all looked alike, with their trees and their warehouses.

She finally stopped in front of a brick building, which I now suspect might have been the old Neuilly tollhouse. But what's the use of trying to find the place? She turned around and stretched her arm toward the back seat, reaching for a Paris map and another object that she showed me and whose purpose I didn't know: a brown crocodile-skin cigarette case.

"Here, Patoche, this is for you . . . It'll come in handy later on."

I contemplated the crocodile-skin case. It had a metal lining inside and contained two sweet-smelling cigarettes made of blond tobacco. I took them out of the case and, as I was about to thank her for the present and hand her back the two cigarettes, I saw her face, in profile. She was staring straight in front of her. A tear was falling down her cheek. I didn't dare make a sound, and Frede's nephew's statement echoed in my head: "Annie cried all night long at Carroll's."

I fondled the cigarette case. I waited. She turned toward me and smiled.

"Do you like it?"

And, with an abrupt movement, she started up. She always made abrupt movements. She always wore men's jackets and pants. Except at night. Her blond hair was very short. But there was such feminine softness about her, and such frailty . . . On the road back, I thought about her serious expression, when she sat with Jean D. in the 4CV under the rain.

I returned to that neighborhood, about twenty years ago, more or less around the time when I'd seen Jean D. again. For the month of July and the month of August, I lived in a tiny room beneath the eaves in Square de Graisivaudan. The sink touched the bed. The foot of the latter was just a few inches from the door and, to enter the room, you had to let yourself topple onto it. I was trying to finish my first book. I walked around the fringes of the sixteenth arrondissement, Neuilly, and Levallois, where Annie used to bring my brother and me on our days off from school. That whole ill-defined zone, which might or might not have still been Paris, and all those streets were wiped off the map when they built the *périphérique*, taking with them all their garages and their secrets.

I didn't think once about Annie when I lived in that neighborhood that we'd driven through together so often. A more distant past haunted me, because of my father.

He had been arrested one February evening in a restaurant on Rue de Marignan. He didn't have his identity papers on him. The police were conducting checks because of a new German regulation prohibiting Jews from being in public places after 8 P.M. He had taken advantage of the twilight and a momentary distraction on the detectives' part at the Black Maria to make his escape.

The following year, they had apprehended him at home. They had taken him to a holding cell, then to an annex of the Drancy transit camp, in Paris, on the Quai de la Gare—a vast merchandise depot where all the Jewish belongings the Germans had looted were being stored: furniture, dishware, linens, toys, carpets, and artworks, arranged by level and section as if in a huge department store. The prisoners emptied the cases as they arrived and filled other cases heading for Germany.

One night, someone showed up in an automobile at the Quai de la Gare and had my father released. I imagined — rightly or wrongly — that it was a certain Louis Pagnon, whom they called "Eddy" and who was shot after the Liberation with members of the Rue Lauriston gang, to which he belonged.

Yes, someone got my father out of the "hole," to use the expression he'd employed one evening when I was fifteen, when I was alone with him and he'd strayed very close to confiding a few things. I felt, that evening, that he would have liked to hand me down his experience of the murky and painful episodes in his life, but that he couldn't find the words. Was it Pagnon or someone else? I needed answers to my questions. What possible connection could there have been between that man and my father? A chance encounter before the war? In the period when I lived in Square de Graisivaudan, I tried to elucidate the mystery by attempting to track down Pagnon. I had gotten authorization to consult the old archives. He was born in Paris, in the tenth arrondissement, between République and the Canal Saint-Martin. My father had also spent his childhood in the tenth arrondissement, but a bit farther over, near the Cité d'Hauteville. Had they met in school? In 1932, Pagnon had received a light sentence from the court of Mont-de-Marsan for "operating a gambling parlor." Between 1937 and 1939, he had worked in a garage in the seventeenth arrondissement. He had known a certain Henri, a sales representative for Simca automobiles, who lived near the Porte des Lilas, and someone named Edmond Delehaye, a foreman at the Savary auto repair in Aubervilliers. The three men got together often; all three worked with cars. The war came, and the Occupation. Henri started a black market operation. Edmond Delehaye acted as his secretary, and Pagnon as driver. They set up shop in a private hotel on Rue Lauriston, near Place de l'Etoile, with a few other unsavory individuals. Those hoods—to use my father's expression—slowly got sucked into the system: from black marketeering, they'd moved into doing the police's dirty work for the Germans.

Pagnon had been involved in a smuggling case that the police report called "the Biarritz stockings affair." It concerned a large quantity of socks that Pagnon collected from various black marketeers in the area. He bundled them in packs of a dozen and dropped them off near the Bayonne train station. They had filled six boxcars with them. In the deserted Paris of the Occupation years, Pagnon drove a fancy car, owned a racehorse, lived in a luxurious furnished apartment on Rue des Belles-Feuilles, and had the wife of a marquis for a mistress. With her, he frequented the riding club in Neuilly, Barbizon, the Fruit Défendu restaurant in Bougival . . . When had my father met Pagnon? At the time of the Biarritz stockings affair? Who can say? One afternoon in 1939, in the seventeenth arrondissement, my father had stopped at a garage to have a tire changed on his Ford, and there was Pagnon. They had chatted awhile; maybe Pagnon had asked him for a favor or some advice. They'd gone off to have a drink at a nearby café with Henri and Edmond Delahaye . . . One meets the strangest people in one's life.

I had hung around the Porte des Lilas, hoping there was still someone who remembered a Simca dealer who'd lived near there around 1939. A certain Henri. But no, it didn't ring any bells for anyone. In Aubervilliers, on Avenue Jean-Jaurès, the Savary repair shop that had employed Edmond Delahaye was long gone. And the garage in the seventeenth arrondissement where Pagnon worked? If I managed to track it down, an old mechanic might tell me about Pagnon and—I hoped—my father. And I would finally know everything I needed to know, everything my father knew.

I had drawn up a list of garages in the seventeenth, preferably those located at the edge of the arrondissement. I had an intuition that Pagnon had worked in one of these:

Garage des Réservoirs
Société Ancienne du Garage-Auto-Star
Van Zon
Vicar and Co.
Villa de l'Auto
Garage Côte d'Azur
Garage Caroline
Champerret-Marly-Automobiles
Cristal Garage
De Korsak
Eden Garage
L'Etoile du Nord
Auto-Sport Garage
Garage Franco-Américain
S.O.C.O.V.A.
Majestic Automobiles
Garage des Villas
Auto-Lux
Garage Saint-Pierre
Garage de la Comète
Garage Bleu
Matford-Automobiles
Diak
Garage du Bois des Caures
As Garage
Dixmude-Palace-Auto
Buffalo-Transports
Duvivier (R) S.A.R.L.
Autos-Remises
Lancien Frère
Garage aux Docks de la Jonquière

Today, I tell myself that the garage where Annie brought me and my brother must be on that list. Perhaps it was the same as Pagnon's. I can still see the leaves on the trees lining the sidewalks, the wide tan pedimented façade . . . They tore it down with the others, and all those years have become, for me, nothing but a long and vain search for a lost garage.

Annie took me to another area of Paris that I later had no trouble recognizing: Avenue Junot, in Montmartre. She parked the 4CV in front of a small white building with a glass-paneled door made of cast iron. She told me to wait. She wouldn't be long. She went into the building.

I walked down the avenue. Perhaps the liking I've always had for that neighborhood comes from then. A sharply vertical flight of steps led to another street below, and I had fun going down it. I walked for a few yards on Rue Caulaincourt, but I never strayed too far. I went back up the steps quickly, afraid that Annie would drive away in her 4CV and leave me behind.

But she wasn't there yet and I had to wait some more, the way we used to wait in the garage, when the orange shade was drawn behind the window of Buck Danny's office. She came out of the building with Roger Vincent. He smiled at me. He pretended to be running into me by chance.

"Well, what do you know . . . Fancy meeting you here!"

For days afterward, he would say to Andrée K., Jean D., or Little Hélène:

"It's funny . . . I ran into Patoche in Montmartre . . . I wonder what he could have been doing there . . ."

And he turned to me:

"Don't breathe a word. The less you say, the better."

On Avenue Junot, Annie kissed him. She called him "Roger Vincent" and used the formal *vous*, but she kissed him.

"Someday I'll have you up to my place," Roger Vincent said to me. "I live here."

And he pointed to the cast-iron front door of the small white building.

The three of us strolled along the sidewalk. His American car wasn't parked in front of his building and I asked him why.

"I keep it in the garage across the way."

We walked past the Hôtel Alsina, near the flight of steps. One time, Annie said:

"That's where I lived, at first, with Little Hélène and Mathilde . . . You should have seen the face Mathilde used to make . . ."

Roger Vincent smiled. And I, without realizing it, absorbed everything they said and their words were etched in my memory.

Much later, I married and lived in that neighborhood for a few years. Almost every day I walked up Avenue Junot. One afternoon, something just came over me: I pushed open the glass-paneled door of the white building. I rang at the concierge's lodge. A red-haired man stuck his head through the opening.

"Can I help you?"

"I'm looking for someone who lived in this building, about twenty years ago . . ."

"Oh, well, I wasn't here then, Monsieur."

"You wouldn't happen to know how I might get some information about him?"

"Go ask at the garage across the street. They used to know everybody."

But I didn't go ask at the garage across the street. I had spent so many years looking for garages in Paris that I no longer believed in them.

In summer the days grew longer, and Annie, who wasn't as strict as Snow White, let us play in the evening in the gently sloping avenue in front of the house. On those evenings we didn't wear our bathrobes. After dinner, Annie walked us to the door and gave me her wristwatch:

"You can play until nine-thirty. At nine-thirty, you're to come in. Keep an eye on the time, Patoche—I'm counting on you."

When Jean D. was there, he would lend me his huge watch. He set it so that at precisely nine-thirty, a little bell—like on an alarm clock—would tell us it was time to go back inside.

The two of us walked down the avenue to the main road where the occasional car was still passing by. A hundred yards away to the right was the train station, a small, weather-beaten, half-timbered structure that looked like a seaside villa. In front of it, a deserted esplanade bordered by trees and the Café de la Gare.

One Thursday, my father didn't come by car with a friend but by train. At the end of the afternoon, the two of us accompanied him to the station. And since we were early, he took us to the terrace of the Café de la Gare. My brother and I had Coca-Colas, and he a brandy.

He had paid the bill and stood up to go catch his train. Before leaving us, he said:

"Don't forget . . . If by chance you see the marquis de Caussade at the chateau, be sure to tell him Albert says hello."

At the corner of the main road and the avenue, protected by a clump of privet hedges, we spied on the station. From time to time, a group of travelers emerged and fanned out toward the town, the water mill on the Bièvre, the Food Hamlet. The travelers grew increasingly scarce. Soon, only one person was left in the esplanade. The marquis de Caussade? That night, for sure, we'd have our big adventure and go up to the chateau. But we knew perfectly well that the plan would always be put off until tomorrow.

We stood still for a long time in front of the hedges that protected the Robin des Bois inn. We eavesdropped on the conversations of diners seated at the tables in the garden. The hedges concealed them, but their voices were very near. We could hear the tinkling of silverware, the waiters' steps crunching on the gravel. The aroma of certain dishes mixed with the scent of privet. But the latter was stronger. The entire avenue smelled like privet.

Up ahead, a light went on in the bow window of the living room. Roger Vincent's American car was parked in front of the house. That evening, he'd come with Andrée K., "the wife of the big-shot doctor," the one who'd been part of the Rue Lauriston gang and who used *tu* with Roger Vincent. It wasn't nine-thirty yet, but Annie emerged from the house, her light blue dress belted at the waist. We crossed the avenue again, as fast as possible, crouching low, and hid behind the bushes of the wooded area next to the Protestant temple. Annie came closer. Her blond hair formed a stain on the twilight. We could hear her footsteps. She was trying to find us. It was a game we played. Each time, we hid in a different spot, in the abandoned lot that the trees and vegetation had taken over. She always ended up finding our hiding place, because we would break out in hysterical laughter when she got too close. The three of us went back to the house. She was a child, like us.

Some sentences remain etched in your mind forever. One afternoon there was a kind of fair in the yard of the Protestant temple, across from the house. From our bedroom window, we had a plunging view of the little stalls around which children crowded with their parents. At lunch, Mathilde had said to me:

"How would you like to go to the festival at the temple, blissful idiot?"

She took us. We bought a lottery ticket and won two packets of nougat. On the way back, Mathilde said:

"They let you in because I'm a Protestant, blissful idiot!"

She was stern as ever, wearing her cameo and black dress.

"And let's get one thing straight: Protestants see everything! There's nothing you can hide from them! They don't only have two eyes—they also have one in the back of their heads! You got that?"

She pointed to her bun.

"You got that, blissful idiot? An eye in the back of our heads!"

From then on, my brother and I felt nervous in her presence, especially when we were passing behind her back. It took me a long time to realize that Protestants were just like anyone else and not to cross the street when I saw one coming.

Never will another sentence have the same resonance for us. It was like Roger Vincent's smile: I've never met one like it. Even in Roger Vincent's absence, that smile floated in the air. I also remember a sentence that Jean D. said. One morning, he had taken me on his motorcycle up to the Versailles road. He wasn't going too fast, and I held on to his Canadienne. On the way back, we stopped at the Robin des Bois inn to buy some cigarettes. The manageress was alone at the bar, a very pretty young blonde who wasn't the one my father had known, back when he'd frequented the inn with Eliot Salter, the marquis de Caussade, and perhaps with Eddy Pagnon.

"A pack of Baltos," Jean D. said.

The manageress handed him the pack of cigarettes, flashing both of us a smile. When we left the inn, Jean D. said to me in a serious voice:

"You know, old man . . . Women . . . They seem great from a distance, but up close, you've got to watch yourself."

He suddenly looked very sad.

One Thursday we were playing on the knoll near the chateau. Little Hélène was watching us, sitting on the bench where Snow White normally sat. We climbed up the branches of the pine trees. I had climbed too high and, while moving from one branch to the next, I nearly fell. When I climbed down from the tree, Little Hélène was pale as a ghost. That day she was wearing her riding breeches and her mother-of-pearl bolero jacket.

"That wasn't smart . . . You could have been killed!"

I had never heard her use such a harsh tone.

"Don't ever do that again!"

I was so unused to seeing her angry that I felt like crying.

"I had to give up my career because of a stupid stunt like that."

She took me by the shoulder and yanked me to the stone bench under the trees. She made me sit down. She took a crocodile-skin wallet from the inside pocket of her bolero jacket—the same color as the cigarette case Annie had given me, presumably from the same store. And from that wallet, she extracted a piece of paper and handed it to me.

"You know how to read?"

It was a newspaper clipping with a photo. I read the headline: TRAPEZE ARTIST HÉLÈNE TOCH IN SERIOUS ACCIDENT. MUSTAPHA AMAR AT HER BEDSIDE. She took back the clipping and returned it to her wallet.

"Accidents can happen very suddenly in life . . . I used to be like you—clueless . . . I was very trusting."

She seemed to have second thoughts about talking to me in such an adult way.

"Come on, let's go have a snack. We'll get something at the pastry shop . . ."

All along Rue du Docteur-Dordaine, I hung back a bit to watch her walk. She had a slight limp. It had never occurred to me before then that she hadn't always limped. So, accidents could happen in life. That revelation troubled me deeply.

■

The afternoon when I'd gone to Paris alone in Annie's 4CV and she had given me the crocodile cigarette case, we had eventually found our way through the small streets, now demolished, of the seventeenth arrondissement. We followed the quays along the Seine, as usual. We stopped for a moment on the riverbank near Neuilly and the Ile de Puteaux. From the top of the wooden stairs that led to the light-colored pontoons, we gazed over the floating houses and barges converted into apartments.

"We're going to have to move soon, Patoche . . . And this is where I want to live . . ."

She had already mentioned this to us, several times. We were a bit worried at the prospect of leaving the house and our town. But to live on one of those barges . . . Day after day, we waited to set off on this new adventure.

"We'll make a room for the two of you. With portholes . . . We'll have a big living room and a bar . . ."

She was musing aloud. We got back into the 4CV. After the Saint-Cloud tunnel, on the highway, she turned toward me. She looked at me with eyes that shone even brighter than usual.

"You know what you should do? Every evening, you should write down what you did that day. I'll buy you a special notebook . . ."

It was a good idea. I stuck my hand in my pocket to reassure myself I still had the cigarette case.

Certain objects disappear from your life at the first lapse in attention, but that cigarette case has remained. I knew it would always be within reach, in a nightstand drawer, on a shelf in a clothes closet, at the back of a desk, in the inner pocket of a jacket. I was so sure of it, of its presence, that I usually forgot all about it. Except when I was feeling down. Then I would ponder it from every angle. It was the only object that bore witness to a period of my life I couldn't talk to anyone about, and whose very reality I sometimes doubted.

Still, I almost lost it one day. I was in one of those schools where I bided my time until the age of seventeen. My cigarette case caught the eye of two twin brothers from the upper bourgeoisie. They had loads of cousins in the other grades, and their father bore the title "top marksman in France." If they all banded against me, I wouldn't stand a chance.

The only way to escape them was to get myself expelled as fast as possible. I ran away one morning, and I took the opportunity to visit Chantilly, Mortefontaine, Ermenonville, and the Abbey of Chaalis. I returned to school at dinnertime. The principal announced my expulsion but he couldn't reach my parents. My father had left for Colombia some time before, to check out a silver mine a friend had told him about; my mother was on tour near La Chaux-de-Fonds. They quarantined me in a room in the nurse's station until someone could come collect me. I wasn't allowed to go to class or take my meals in the dining hall with my schoolmates. This kind of diplomatic immunity kept me safe from the two brothers, their cousins, and the top marksman in France. Every night before going to sleep, I verified the presence under my pillow of the crocodile cigarette case.

The object drew attention to itself one more time, a few years later. I had ended up taking Annie's advice to write in a notebook, every day: I had just finished my first novel. I was sitting at the bar of a café on Avenue de Wagram. Next to me stood a man of about sixty with black hair, wearing glasses with very slender frames, whose appearance was as immaculate as his hands. For several minutes I'd been watching him, wondering what he did in life.

He had asked the waiter for a pack of cigarettes, but they didn't sell any in that café. I offered my crocodile-skin case.

"Much obliged, Monsieur."

He extracted a cigarette. His gaze remained fixed on the crocodile case.

"May I?"

He plucked it from my hand and turned it over and over, knitting his brow.

"I used to have the same one."

He handed it back and looked at me more closely.

"They stole our entire stock of this item. Afterward we stopped carrying it. You have here a very rare collector's item . . ."

He smiled. He had managed a fine leather goods shop on the Champs-Elysées, but was now retired.

"They weren't satisfied with just those cases. They emptied the entire store."

He leaned his face closer to mine, still smiling.

"You needn't think I suspect you in the slightest . . . You would have been too young at the time."

"Was it that long ago?" I asked.

"A good fifteen years."

"And were they ever caught?"

"Not all of them. Those people had done things much more serious than breaking and entering."

Things much more serious. I already knew those words. The trapeze artist Hélène Toch in a SERIOUS ACCIDENT. And later, the young man with large blue eyes had told me: SOMETHING VERY SERIOUS.

Outside, on Avenue de Wagram, I walked with a curious euphoria in my heart. It was the first time in a long while that I felt Annie's presence. She was walking behind me that evening. Roger Vincent and Little Hélène must also have been somewhere in the city. In the final account, they had never left me.

Snow White disappeared for good without giving notice. At lunch, Mathilde said:

"She left because she couldn't stand looking after you, blissful idiot!"

Annie shrugged her shoulders and winked at me.

"That's a stupid thing to say, Mom! She left because she had to go back to her family."

Mathilde squinted and gave her daughter a nasty look.

"You don't talk to your mother that way in front of the children!"

Annie pretended not to listen. She smiled at us.

"Did you hear me?" Mathilde said to her daughter. "You'll come to a bad end, just like Blissful Idiot here!"

Annie shrugged again.

"Take it easy, Thilda," said Little Hélène.

Mathilde looked at me and pointed to the bun on the back of her head.

"You know what that means, don't you? Now that Snow White is gone, *I'll* be looking after you, blissful idiot!"

Annie walked me to school. She had put her hand on my shoulder, as usual.

"Don't pay any attention to what Mom says . . . She's old. Old people talk nonsense."

We had arrived early. We waited in front of the iron gate to the playground.

"You and your brother are going to sleep for a night or two in the house across the street . . . you know, the white one. We're having some people come live at our house for a few days . . ."

She must have noticed my worried look.

"And anyway, I'll be staying with you . . . You'll see, it'll be fun."

In class, I couldn't concentrate on the lesson. My mind was elsewhere. Snow White had gone, and now we were going to live in the house across the street.

After school, Annie took my brother and me to the house across the street. She rang at the small door that opened onto Rue du Docteur-Dordaine. A brown-haired woman, rather corpulent and dressed in black, opened for us. She was the housekeeper, as the owners of the place never lived there.

"The room's all ready," said the housekeeper.

We went up a flight of stairs lit by electric lights. All the shutters in the house were closed. We followed a hallway. The housekeeper opened a door. The room was larger than ours, and there were two beds with brass bars, two grown-up beds. The walls were covered in light blue patterned wallpaper. A window looked out onto Rue du Docteur-Dordaine: those shutters were open.

"You'll like it here, kids," said Annie.

The housekeeper smiled at us. She said:

"I'll make you breakfast in the morning."

We went back down the stairs, and the housekeeper showed us the ground floor of the house. In the large living room, with its closed shutters, two crystal chandeliers shone bright enough to blind us. The furniture was cased in transparent slipcovers. Except for the piano.

After dinner, we went out with Annie. We were wearing our pajamas and our bathrobes. A spring evening. It was fun to wear our bathrobes outside, and we walked down the avenue with Annie, all the way to the Robin des Bois inn. We wished we would run into someone so they'd see us walking around in our bathrobes.

We rang at the door of the house across the street and, once again, the housekeeper opened up and took us to our room. We got into the beds with the brass bars. The housekeeper told us her bedroom was downstairs, next to the living room, and we could call her if there was anything we needed.

"And anyway, Patoche, I'm right nearby," said Annie.

She gave us each a kiss on the forehead. We had already brushed our teeth after dinner, in our real room. The housekeeper closed the shutters and turned off the light, and the two of them went out.

That first night, we talked for a long time, my brother and I. We would have loved to go downstairs to the living room on the ground floor to look at the chandeliers, the chairs in their slipcases, and the piano, but we were afraid the wood of the staircase would creak and the housekeeper would scold us.

The next morning was Thursday. I had no school. The housekeeper brought us breakfast in our room, on a tray. We said thank you.

Frede's nephew didn't come that Thursday. We stayed in the large garden, near the façade of the house with its French doors and closed shutters. There was a weeping willow and, way in back, a bamboo wall through which we could make out the terrace of the Robin des Bois inn and the tables that the waiters were setting for dinner. We ate sandwiches at noon. The housekeeper made them for us. We were sitting in the garden chairs with our sandwiches, as if for a picnic. That evening the weather was warm, and we had dinner in the garden. The housekeeper had again made us ham and cheese sandwiches. Two apple tarts for dessert. And Coca-Cola.

Annie came round after dinner. We'd put on our pajamas and bathrobes. We went out with her. This time, we crossed the main road at the bottom of the hill. We met some people near the public garden, and they looked surprised to see us in our bathrobes. Annie was wearing her old leather jacket and her blue jeans. We walked past the train station. It occurred to me that we could take the train, in our bathrobes, all the way to Paris.

When we returned, Annie kissed us in the garden of the white house and gave each of us a harmonica.

I woke up in the middle of the night. I heard the rumble of a car engine. I got up and went to the window. The housekeeper hadn't closed the shutters, just drawn the red curtains.

Across the street, a light was on in the bow window of the living room. Roger Vincent's car was parked in front of the house, its black convertible top folded down. Annie's 4CV was there too. But the sound of the motor came from a canvas-covered truck idling on the other side of the street, near the wall of the Protestant temple. The motor shut off. Two men came out of the truck. I recognized Jean D. and Buck Danny, and the two of them went into the house. Now and then I saw a silhouette pass in front of the bow window of the living room. I was sleepy. The next morning, the housekeeper woke us carrying the tray with our breakfast. She and my brother took me to school. On Rue du Docteur-Dordaine, there was no sign of the truck or Roger Vincent's car. But Annie's 4CV was still there, in front of the house.

When I got out of school, my brother was waiting for me all alone. "There's nobody home at our house."

He told me the housekeeper had brought him back to the house a little while ago. Annie's 4CV was there, but no one was home. The housekeeper had to go do the shopping in Versailles until late that afternoon and she had left my brother at the house, telling him that Annie would be back soon since her car was there. My brother had sat in the empty house, waiting.

He looked happy to see me. He even laughed, like someone who had been afraid but was now relieved.

"They just went to Paris," I reassured him. "Don't you worry."

We walked up Rue du Docteur-Dordaine. Annie's 4CV was there.

Nobody in the dining room or the kitchen. Or the living room. Upstairs, Annie's room was empty. Little Hélène's as well. So was Mathilde's, in the back of the courtyard. We went into Snow White's room: maybe she had come back after all. But no. It was as if no one had ever lived in those rooms. Through the window of our bedroom, I stared down at Annie's 4CV.

The silence in the house was frightening. I turned on the radio and we ate the two apples and two bananas that remained in the fruit basket, on the sideboard. I opened the back door. The green bumper car was still there, in the middle of the courtyard.

"We'll wait for them," I said to my brother.

Time passed. The hands on the kitchen clock said twenty minutes to two. It was time to go back to school. But I couldn't leave my brother all alone. We sat down, facing each other, at the dining room table. We listened to the radio.

We went outside. Annie's 4CV was still there. I opened one of the doors and sat in the front seat, in my usual spot. I rifled through the glove compartment and carefully inspected the back seat. Nothing. Except an empty cigarette pack.

"Let's walk up to the chateau," I said to my brother.

The wind was blowing. We walked along Rue du Docteur-Dordaine. My friends were already back in school, and the teacher would have noticed my absence. The more we walked, the deeper the silence grew around us. Beneath the sun, that street and all its houses seemed deserted.

The wind gently ruffled the tall grass in the meadow. The two of us had never ventured here alone. The boarded-up windows of the chateau provoked the same anxiety in me as in the evenings, coming back from our walks in the woods with Snow White. The chateau façade was dark and threatening in those moments. As it was now, in midafternoon.

We sat down on the bench, where Snow White and Little Hélène used to sit back when we climbed the branches of the pine trees. The silence still hovered around us, and I tried to play a tune on the harmonica Annie had given me.

On Rue du Docteur-Dordaine, we saw, from afar, a black car parked in front of the house. A man was at the wheel, his leg sticking out from the open driver's-side door, and he was reading the newspaper. At the door to the house, a gendarme in uniform stood very stiff, with a bare head. He was young, with short-cropped blond hair, and his big blue eyes stared into the void.

He started and looked at my brother and me, his eyes wide.

"What are you doing here?"

"This is my house," I said. "Has something happened?"

"Something very serious."

I felt afraid. But his voice was trembling a bit as well. A truck with a crane turned the corner of the avenue. A bunch of gendarmes hopped out and attached Annie's 4CV to the crane. Then the truck started up again, slowly towing Annie's 4CV behind it down Rue du Docteur-Dordaine. That was the part that hit me hardest and made me feel the worst.

"It's very serious," he said. "You can't go in."

But we did go in. Someone was on the phone in the living room. A dark-haired man in a gabardine coat was sitting on the edge of the dining room table. He saw my brother and me and came toward us.

"Ah . . . Are you them? . . . The children . . . ?"

He repeated:

"Are you the children?"

He pulled us into the living room. The man on the phone hung up. He was short with very wide shoulders, and he wore a black leather jacket. He said, like the other one:

"Ah . . . It's the children."

He said to the man in the gabardine coat:

"You'll have to take them to headquarters in Versailles. Nobody's answering in Paris . . ."

Something very serious, the gendarme with the big blue eyes had said. I remembered the newspaper clipping that Little Hélène kept in her wallet: TRAPEZE ARTIST HÉLÈNE TOCH IN SERIOUS ACCIDENT. I kept behind her to watch her walk. She hadn't always had that limp.

"Where are your parents?" the dark-haired man in the gabardine coat asked me.

I tried to find an answer. It was too complicated to explain. Annie had said so, the day when we'd gone together to see the principal of the Jeanne d'Arc school and she'd pretended to be my mother.

"Don't you know where your parents are?"

My mother was acting in her play somewhere in North Africa. My father was in Brazzaville or Bangui, or somewhere farther still. It was too complicated.

"They're dead," I told him.

He flinched. He looked at me, knitting his brow. It was as if he was suddenly afraid of me. The short man in the leather jacket stared at me as well, with worried eyes, his lips parted. Two gendarmes entered the living room.

"Should we keep searching the house?" one of them asked the dark-haired man in the gabardine coat.

"Yes, yes . . . Keep searching . . ."

They left. The dark-haired man in the gabardine coat leaned toward us.

"Go play in the garden," he said in a very gentle voice. "I'll come see you in a little bit."

He took each of us by the hand and led us outside. The green bumper car was still there. He stretched out his arm toward the garden:

"Go play . . . I'll see you in a little bit."

And he went back inside the house.

We climbed the stone steps to the first terrace of the garden, where the grave of Doctor Guillotin was hidden under the clematis and Mathilde had planted a rose bush. The window to Annie's room was wide open, and since we were level with that window, I could see that they were searching everything in Annie's room.

Lower down, the short man in the black leather jacket was crossing the courtyard, holding a flashlight. He leaned over the edge of the well, pushed aside the honeysuckle and strained to see something down at the bottom, with his flashlight. The others continued rummaging through Annie's room. Still others arrived, gendarmes and men wearing everyday clothes. They searched everywhere, even inside our bumper car; they walked around the courtyard, appeared in the windows of the house, and called to each other in loud voices. And my brother and I, we pretended to play in the garden, waiting for someone to come collect us.

FLOWERS OF RUIN

For Zina
For Marie
For Douglas

> A chatty old woman
> A rider in gray
> An ass that is watching
> A rope fall away
> Some lilies and roses
> In an old mustard pot
> On the highway to Paris
> These things you will spot.

> —Lamartine

That Sunday evening in November, I was on Rue de l'Abbé-de-l'Epée. I was skirting the high wall around the Institut des Sourds-Muets. To the left rises the bell tower of the church of Saint-Jacques-du-Haut-Pas. I could still recall a café at the corner of Rue Saint-Jacques, where I used to go after taking in a film at the Studio des Ursulines.

On the sidewalk, dead leaves. Or burned pages from an old Gaffiot dictionary. It's the neighborhood of colleges and convents. My memory dredged up a few outdated names: Estrapade, Contrescarpe, Tournefort, Pot-de-Fer . . . I felt apprehensive crossing through places where I hadn't set foot since I was eighteen, when I attended a lycée on the Montagne-Sainte-Geneviève.

Those areas looked the same to me as when I'd last seen them in the early sixties, as if they'd been abandoned at around the same time, more than twenty-five years ago. On Rue Gay-Lussac — that quiet street where once they'd pried up the cobblestones and erected barricades — the door of a hotel was boarded up and most of the windows were missing their panes. But the sign remained affixed to the wall: Hôtel de l'Avenir. Hotel of the Future. What future? The one, already past, of a student from the 1930s who took a small room in that hotel after graduating from the Ecole Normale Supérieure, and who on Saturday nights would have his friends over. They would go around the corner to watch a film at the Studio des Ursulines. I walked by the gate and the white shuttered building, in which the cinema occupies the ground floor. The entryway was lit. I could have walked to the Val-de-Grâce, in that peaceful zone where we had hidden,

Jacqueline and I, so that the marquis would have no chance of finding her. We lived in a hotel at the end of Rue Pierre-Nicole. We subsisted on the money Jacqueline had gotten from selling her fur coat. The sundrenched street on Sunday afternoons. The privet hedges of the small brick building opposite the Collège Sévigné. The hotel balconies were covered in ivy. The dog napped in the entrance hall.

I reached Rue d'Ulm. It was deserted. Though I kept telling myself that there was nothing unusual about that on a Sunday evening in this studious, provincial neighborhood, I wondered whether I was still in Paris. In front of me, the dome of the Pantheon. It frightened me to be there alone, at the foot of that funereal monument in the moonlight, and I veered off into Rue Lhomond. I stopped in front of the Collège des Irlandais. A bell tolled eight o'clock, perhaps the one at the Congrégation du Saint-Esprit, whose massive façade rose to my right. A few more steps and I emerged onto Place de l'Estrapade. I looked for number 26 on Rue des Fossés-Saint-Jacques. A modern building rose before me. The old one had probably been torn down a good twenty years earlier.

April 24, 1933. A young married couple commits suicide for no apparent reason.

It's a very strange story that occurred that night in the building at number 26 Rue des Fossés-Saint-Jacques, near the Pantheon, in the home of Mr. and Mme T.

Three years earlier, Monsieur Urbain T., a young engineer, top in his class, had married Mademoiselle Gisèle S., age twenty-six, one year his senior. Mme T. was a pretty blonde, tall and svelte. As for her husband, he was the typical dark and handsome young man. The previous July, the couple had set up house on the ground floor of 26 Rue des Fossés-Saint-Jacques, in a former workshop that they had converted into a studio apartment. The young newlyweds were very close. Nothing seemed to be clouding their happiness.

One Saturday evening, Urbain T. decided to take his wife out to dinner. They both left the house at around seven. They wouldn't return home until about two in the morning, along with two couples they'd just met. The unusual din from their apartment woke the neighbors, unaccustomed to such a racket from tenants who were ordinarily so quiet. No doubt the party took a few unexpected turns.

At around four in the morning, the guests departed. During the half-hour that then passed in silence, two muffled explosions sounded. At nine o'clock, a neighbor, leaving her own apartment, passed in front of the couple's door. She heard moaning. Suddenly remembering the shots heard in the night, she grew worried and knocked. The door opened to reveal Gisèle T. Blood was slowly leaking from a visible wound beneath her left breast. She murmured, "My husband! My husband! Dead." A few moments later, Detective Magnan of the local police appeared on the scene. Gisèle T. was moaning, lying on the couch. In the next room, they discovered the body of her husband. The latter was still clutching a revolver in his hand. He had shot a bullet straight through his heart.

Beside him, a scribbled note: *My wife killed self. We were drunk. I kill self. Don't try . . .*

From the police report, it appears that Urbain and Gisèle T., after their dinner out, found their way to a bar in Montparnasse. The other evening, from Rue des Fossés-Saint-Jacques, I walked to the intersection where the Dôme and the Rotonde stand, after leaving behind the dark gardens of the Observatoire. The T.'s must have followed the same path, that night in 1933. I was surprised to find myself in a place I'd avoided since the early sixties. Like the Studio des Ursulines, the Montparnasse neighborhood always reminded me of Sleeping Beauty's castle. I had felt the same thing at age twenty, when I spent a few nights in a hotel on Rue Delambre: Montparnasse already seemed like a quarter that had outlived itself and was slowly decaying, far from Paris. When it rained on Rue d'Odessa or Rue du Départ, I felt as if I were in a Breton port in the drizzle. The old train station, which hadn't yet been demolished, exhaled gusts of Brest or Lorient. Here, the party had long been over. I remember that the sign for the long-vanished Jimmy's was still clinging to the wall on Rue Huyghens, and that it was missing two or three letters which the sea breezes had blown away.

It was the first time — according to the newspapers in April 1933 — that the young couple had set foot in a Montparnasse nightspot. Had they had a bit too much to drink with dinner? Or else, quite simply, had they felt like disrupting, if only for a night, the tranquil course of their lives? One witness swore he'd seen them at around ten o'clock in the Café de la Marine, a dance hall at 243 Boulevard Raspail; another, at the Cabaret des Isles on Rue Vavin, in the company of two women. The detectives showed their photos around to solicit statements, which had to be taken with a grain of salt, since one saw plenty of blonde girls with dark-haired boys, like Urbain and Gisèle T. For several days they tried to identify the two couples that the T.'s had brought home with them to Rue des Fossés-Saint-Jacques, then the investigation was closed. Gisèle T. had been able to talk before succumbing to her injuries, but her memories were hazy. Yes, they had met two women in Montparnasse, two strangers she didn't know much about . . . And those two had taken them out to Le Perreux, to a dance hall where two men had joined them. Then they'd gone to a house with a red elevator.

This evening, I'm following in their footsteps in a sullen quarter that the Tour Montparnasse veils in mourning. During the day, it hides the sun and throws its shadow onto Boulevard Edgar-Quinet and the surrounding streets. I leave behind me the Coupole, which they're smothering under a concrete façade. It's hard to believe that Montparnasse used to have any nightlife . . .

In what period, exactly, did I live in that hotel on Rue Delambre? Around 1965, when I met Jacqueline, not long before my departure for Vienna.

The room next to mine was occupied by a man of about thirty-five, a blond fellow I'd sometimes meet in the hall and who I ended up getting to know. His name? Something like Devez or Duvelz.

He was always nattily dressed and wore an official decoration on his lapel. Sometimes he invited me out for a drink, at a bar right near the hotel, the Rosebud. I didn't dare refuse. He seemed enchanted with the place.

"It's very pleasant here . . ."

He spoke from the tip of his teeth, with the voice of a well-heeled scion. He confided to me that he'd spent more than three years "in the djebel" and that he'd earned his decoration over there. But the Algerian War had sickened him. He'd needed a long time to get over it. Very soon he was going to take over for his father as head of a large textile concern in the North.

It didn't take me long to realize he wasn't telling the whole truth: about that "large textile concern," he remained vague. And he contradicted himself, telling me one day that he'd graduated from Saint-Maixent, just before his departure for Algeria, then the next day that he'd done all his schooling in England. Sometimes his plummy dental accent yielded to a street hawker's patter.

It was only because I was walking in Montparnasse that Sunday evening that Duvelz—or Devez—suddenly reemerged from the void. I remembered that one day, we had run into each other on Rue de Rennes, and he had invited me for a stein of beer, as he said, at one of those dismal cafés in Place Saint-Placide.

The Cabaret des Isles on Rue Vavin, where the couple had allegedly been spotted, occupied the basement of Les Vikings. The Scandinavian ambiance and light-colored wood of Les Vikings clashed with the Negro cabaret. You just had to go downstairs: from the Norwegian cocktails and hors-d'oeuvres of the ground floor, you were plunged into the frenzy of Martinican dances. Is that where the T.'s met the two women? I suspect it was instead at the Café de la Marine on Boulevard Raspail, near Denfert-Rochereau. I remember the apartment where Duvelz had dragged Jacqueline and me, at one end of that same Boulevard Raspail. I hadn't dared refuse his invitation that time, either. For nearly a week, he had insisted that the two of us come on Saturday evening to visit a woman friend of his that he absolutely wanted us to meet.

She opened the door and, in the half-light of the vestibule, I couldn't quite make out her face. I was struck by the opulence of the large living room we entered, so out of character with Duvelz's small hotel room on Rue Delambre. He was there. He introduced us. I've forgotten her name: a brunette with regular features. One of her cheeks bore a large scar, near the cheekbone.

Jacqueline and I were sitting on the sofa. Duvelz and the woman, on armchairs, facing us. She must have been about Duvelz's age: thirty-five. She looked at us with curiosity.

"Don't you find the two of them charming?" said Duvelz in his dental accent.

She stared fixedly at us. She asked:

"Would you like something to drink?"

Things felt awkward. She served some port.

Duvelz took a large sip.

"Relax," he said. "She's an old friend . . ."

She gave us a shy smile.

"We were even engaged once. But she had to marry someone else . . ."

She didn't react. She sat very straight in her chair, her glass in her hand.

"Her husband is often away. We can take advantage to go out, just the four of us. What do you say?"

"Go out where?" asked Jacqueline.

"Wherever you like. Or we don't have to go out at all."

He shrugged.

"We're perfectly comfortable here . . . No?"

She still sat very stiffly in her chair. She lit a cigarette, perhaps to hide her nervousness. Duvelz swallowed another gulp of port. He put his glass down on the coffee table. He stood up and walked over to her.

"She's pretty, don't you think?"

He ran his index finger over the scar on her cheek. Then he undid her blouse and began fondling her breasts. She didn't react.

"We were in a very serious car accident together, back in the day," he said.

She pushed his hand away gruffly. She smiled at us again.

"You must be hungry . . ."

She had a husky voice and, I thought, a slight accent.

"Will you help me bring dinner in?" she asked him curtly.

"Of course."

The two of them got up.

"It's a cold supper," she said. "Will that be all right?"

"That's perfect," said Jacqueline.

He had taken the woman by the shoulder and steered her out of the living room. He stuck his head through the doorway.

"You like champagne?"

He had lost his dental accent.

"Very much," said Jacqueline.

"Be right back."

We sat alone in the living room for a few minutes, and I'm racking my brains to remember as many details as I can. The French windows looking out on the boulevard were half-open because of the heat. It was at 19 Boulevard Raspail. In 1965. A grand piano at the very back of the room. The sofa and the two armchairs were made of the same black leather. The coffee table of chrome-plated metal. A name like Devez or Duvelz. The scar on the cheek. The unbuttoned blouse. A very bright light, as if from a projector, or rather a flashlight. It lights only a portion of the scene, an isolated instant, leaving the rest in shadow. We will never know what happened next or who those two people really were.

We slipped out of the living room and, without shutting the door behind us, crept down the stairs. Earlier, we had taken the elevator, but it wasn't red like the one mentioned by Gisèle T.

A statement by a waiter who worked in a restaurant-nightclub in Le Perreux figures on the front page of an evening paper in that month of April 1933. The headline is as follows:

POLICE SEARCHING FOR TWO COUPLES
WHO SPENT EVENING IN APARTMENT
OF YOUNG CHEMIST AND HIS WIFE

At police headquarters in the Val-de-Grâce precinct, though the investigation has been called off because it was ruled a double suicide, they tell us that the young couple had gone not only to Montparnasse but also to the banks of the Marne, to Le Perreux; and that they went not just with two women but with two women and two men. . . . Attempts to locate these four individuals have so far been in vain.

We went to Le Perreux in hopes of gleaning a few important details on the moments preceding the tragedy.

In a "restaurant-nightclub" on the Quai de l'Artois, they clearly remember the presence of the two young persons.

"They arrived at around ten," states the waiter who served them. "They were alone. She was very pretty, blonde, very slim . . . They were sitting over there, under the balcony. Is that where they met the people they invited home? I didn't notice. We get a lot of traffic on Saturday nights at that time of year. They didn't seem to be having an especially good time. In any case, I remember they settled their check at eleven-thirty."

It is hard to take this testimony at face value, as it presupposes that the T.'s had gone to Le Perreux alone, and of their own accord. But everything we know about their life in the quiet neighborhood around Rue des Fossés-Saint-Jacques suggests that they were not the type to frequent dance halls on the banks of the Marne on Saturday nights. No, it was certainly the two unknown women, met in Montparnasse, who took them to Le Perreux that night, as Gisèle T. had herself indicated. And one has to wonder why the waiter made such a statement. Did he confuse them with other customers? More likely, he was trying to steer the investigators away from the people in whose company he had seen the T.'s, two women and two men, no doubt regulars of the establishment. The two women from Montparnasse knew the two men. But where—asked the newspaper article—was the house with the red elevator that Gisèle T. had spoken of?

Leaving the Café de la Marine, the T.'s and the two unknown women might have taken a taxi. But no cab driver, the day after the tragedy, told investigators that he'd driven four fares to Le Perreux-sur-Marne. Nor had a single one come forward to say that he'd brought back several couples from Le Perreux to number 26 Rue des Fossés-Saint-Jacques at around two in the morning.

In those days, one went from Paris to Nogent-sur-Marne and Le Perreux via the train station at Bastille or the Gare de l'Est. The trains leaving from Bastille followed the so-called Vincennes line, up to Verneuil-L'Etang. I knew that line even in the early sixties, before the RER replaced it and the Bastille train station was demolished to make way for the new Opera.

The tracks ran along the viaduct on Avenue Daumesnil, whose arches were populated with cafés, warehouses, and businesses. Why do I so often walk along this viaduct in my dreams? This is what one discovered under its arches, in the shade of the plane trees along the avenue:

L'Armanite Laboratory
Garage des Voûtes
Peyremorte
Corrado Casadei
Notre-Dame-de-Lourdes Dispensary
Dell'Aversano
La Régence, furniture maker
Les Marbres Français

Café Bosc
Alligator, Ghesquière and Co.
Sava Autos
Daumesnil Wireworks
Café Labatie
La Radieuse heating
Testas, nonferrous metals
Café-Tabac Valadier

One summer evening, at Café Bosc, just before my departure for Vienna, the tables were set out on the sidewalk. I couldn't take my eyes off the lights of the Gare de Lyon, nearby . . .

The train stopped at Reuilly, then at Bel-Air. It exited Paris via the Porte Montempoivre. It passed by the Braille school and made a stop at Saint-Mandé station, near the lake. Then it was Vincennes, and the station at Nogent-sur-Marne, at the edge of the forest.

From Nogent station, they would have had to walk all the way up Grande Rue to the town of Le Perreux. Unless the two men came to pick them up in a car.

It seems more likely that when leaving the Café de la Marine with the two women, they headed down into the Raspail metro stop, a few yards away from the café.

The metro runs directly to the Gare de l'Est. There, they took the train on the Mulhouse line. When it left Paris, crossing the Canal Saint-Denis, one could see, from above, the slaughterhouses of La Villette. The train stopped in Pantin. Then it ran along the Canal de l'Ourcq. Noisy-le-Sec, Rosny-sous-Bois. They arrived at Le Perreux station. They stepped onto the platform and the train continued on its way, over the viaduct that crosses the Marne River. The two women took them to a restaurant-nightclub right nearby, on the Quai de l'Artois. They were now a group of six, including the two unknown men.

I remember the Quai de l'Artois, which began at the foot of the viaduct. Just opposite was the Ile des Loups. During the years 1964 and 1965, I went to that island: a certain Claude Bernard, to whom I'd sold a music box and several old books, had invited my girlfriend, Jacqueline, and me there several times. He lived in a kind of chalet, with bow windows and verandas. One afternoon, he photographed us on one of the verandas, to try out his new camera, and a few moments later he handed us the color image: it was the first time I'd ever seen a Polaroid.

This Claude Bernard was about forty years old and made his living as a dealer in secondhand goods: he owned warehouses, a stall at the Saint-Ouen flea market, and even a used bookstore on Avenue de Clichy, which is where I'd first met him. After dinner, he drove Jacqueline and me back to Paris in a gray Jaguar. A few years later, I lost touch with him for good. His stall at the flea market and his bookstore on Avenue de Clichy had vanished into thin air. The phone number to his house on the Ile des Loups was "no longer in service."

I'm thinking of him because of the Ile des Loups. In one of the articles about what the newspapers labeled "the tragic orgy," they hinted that the police might have identified one of the unknown men that the T.'s and the two women had met in the restaurant-nightclub on the Quai de l'Artois: a resident of Le Perreux. As far as I'm concerned, he could only have lived on the Ile des Loups. And given the waiter's dubious testimony, I wonder whether the T.'s and the two other couples even went to the restaurant-nightclub on the Quai de l'Artois that evening. It seems more likely that one of the men took them to the Ile des Loups, for that was where the house with the red elevator stood.

Today I'm trying to reconstruct the layout, but at the time when I went to visit Claude Bernard, I would never have imagined such a thing. Claude Bernard had not lived long in that large chalet decorated with verandas and bow windows. A wooden kiosk rose in the back of the garden.

Who had the previous owner been? A certain Jacques Henley? Henley's photo figures in old film directories, with the caption "Speaks English and German without an accent." A very British face: blond mustache, very pale eyes. His address is given as: Jacques Henley, "Les Raquettes," Ile des Loups, Nogent-sur-Marne (Seine), Tremblay 12-00. But in the phone book, at the same telephone number, he is listed under the name E. J. Dothée. Among the other former inhabitants of the island that I was able to inventory:

Willame, H.	Tremblay 33-44
Magnant, L.	Tremblay 22-65

Dothée alias Henley and the two above-mentioned persons lived in the part of the island that belongs to Nogent-sur-Marne; these others lived in the eastern part, in Le Perreux:

Hevelle	Tremblay 11-97
Verchère, E. L., Les Heures	
Tranquilles, Ile des Loups	
(May to Oct.)	Tremblay 09-25
Kisseloff, P.	Tremblay 09-25
Korsak (de)	Tremblay 27-19
Ryan (Jean E.), La Pergola,	
Ile des Loups	Tremblay 06-69

The Société d'Encouragement du Sport Nautique (Tremblay 00-80) was in the part belonging to Nogent-sur-Marne. I believe Claude

Bernard's house, for its part, was located in the eastern sector, part of Le Perreux. In short, the Ile des Loups called to mind that island in the Caribbean split between two countries, Haiti and the Dominican Republic—the difference being that it hadn't won its independence, since it was under the sovereignty of Nogent and Le Perreux. The viaduct crossed through it, and this was what marked the boundary of the two zones.

Clumps of trees lining the banks concealed Claude Bernard's house. He came to get us at the Quai de l'Artois in a small boat. The neglected garden was surrounded by a white fence. On the ground floor, a huge space that opened onto the veranda acted as the living room: a sofa, two leather armchairs, a coffee table, and a large brick fireplace. Claude Bernard was always alone in that house and gave the impression of camping out in it. When he invited us to dinner, he did the cooking himself. He had told me he was tired of living in Paris and that he couldn't sleep without country air, and water nearby.

I suppose there's no trace of countryside left in Le Perreux and on the Ile des Loups. They've no doubt razed Claude Bernard's house. The trees and pontoon boats have disappeared from along the banks.

At the time of our first meeting, in his bookstore on Avenue de Clichy, the day when I offered him the twenty-volume set of Balzac's complete works—the Veuve Houssiaux edition—and he had bought it from me for three thousand francs, we talked literature. He'd confided that his favorite writer was Buffon.

The works of Buffon bound in green morocco leather on the brick mantelpiece of his living room were the only books I noticed at his house. Naturally, that house on the Ile des Loups seemed strange to me, and I found Claude Bernard's occupation as a dealer in "second-hand goods" intriguing. But most often we talked about film or literature, and that's what he liked about me.

I remember the heavy wood paneling on the living room walls, the ironwork, but especially the elevator lined with red velvet—it no longer worked—that Claude Bernard, one day, laughingly told us had been installed by the former owner for the sole purpose of going up to his bedroom on the next floor.

That elevator was the only remaining clue to the night in April 1933 when the T.'s had ended up in Le Perreux with the two other couples. Afterward, they had returned to their sober quarters on Rue des Fossés-Saint-Jacques, but it no longer mattered. It was too late. Their fate had been sealed in Le Perreux and in the house on the Ile des Loups.

At the time, I didn't really care about the whys and wherefores of "the tragic orgy," or about the role of the red velvet elevator that Claude Bernard had shown us at the back of the living room. To us, the Ile des Loups and its environs were just one more suburb. On the route we took from the station to the Quai de l'Artois, where Claude Bernard was waiting for us in his boat, I was thinking that we'd soon be going away, thanks to the money from the Balzacs and the old music box I'd sold him. Before long, Jacqueline and I would be far away from the Marne and Le Perreux—in Vienna, where I'd turn twenty.

I'd like to linger on the Left Bank a while longer, being a child of Saint-Germain-des-Prés. I attended the public school on Rue du Pont-de-Lodi and studied catechism with Father Pachaud on Rue de l'Abbaye and Place Furstenberg. Since then, however, I've avoided my former village, which I no longer recognize. This evening, the Carrefour de l'Odéon seems as desolate to me as the Breton port of Montparnasse in the drizzle.

One of my last memories of Saint-Germain-des-Prés goes back to Monday, January 18, 1960. I was fourteen and a half and I had run away from school. I had walked all the way to La Croix de Berny, skirting the hangars of the Villacoublay airfield. Then I'd taken a bus to the Porte d'Orléans, and then the metro. I had gotten off at Saint-Germain-des-Prés. I ended up in a café, Chez Malafosse, at the end of Rue Bonaparte where it meets the quay. At least, Chez Malafosse is what my father used to call it. After lunch, we'd be in his office with his friends and he'd say to me:

"Go get us some Partagas at Malafosse."

That afternoon, at Chez Malafosse, a group of people my mother knew, who were always hanging about in that neighborhood, were standing at the bar. Among them was a pretty Danish girl with short blond hair and periwinkle eyes. She used slang words that clashed with her soft, childlike accent. Slang that was often outmoded. When she saw me come in, she said:

"What the fuck are you doing here, old top?"

I confessed that I was playing hooky. There was an embarrassed silence. I was on the verge of bursting into tears. Suddenly, she said, with her Danish accent:

"What the fuck does that matter, old top?"

Then she slammed the palm of her hand down on the counter:

"A whiskey for Old Top here . . ."

I recall the billiards players upstairs at the Café de Cluny. I happened to be there, one Saturday afternoon in January, the day of Churchill's funeral. It was in 1966 that they renovated all the cafés on Place Saint-Michel and the boulevard; in recent years, some became McDonald's, like the Mahieu, where the off-track bettors used to gather, and where one could hear the crackling of the machine as it spewed out the racing results.

Until the late sixties, the neighborhood had remained unchanged. The events of May '68, which it hosted, left only black-and-white news images, which at a quarter-century's remove seem as distant as the ones filmed during the Liberation of Paris.

Boulevard Saint-Michel is engulfed in a December-like fog this Sunday evening, and the image of a street resurfaces in my memory, one of the few streets in the Latin Quarter—the only one, I think—that often figures in my dreams. I finally identified it. It slopes gently down to the boulevard, and the contagion of dreams into reality ensures that Rue Cujas will always remain frozen for me in the light of the early sixties, a soft, limpid light that I associate with two films from that time: *Lola* and *Adieu Philippine*.

Toward the bottom of the street, on the ground floor of a hotel, there used to be a movie theater, the Studio Cujas. One July afternoon I entered the cool and darkness of that theater, out of idleness, and I was the only spectator.

A bit farther up, on the Montagne-Sainte-Geneviève, I used to meet a girl I knew who acted in New Wave films—as we called them then.

I thought about her yesterday afternoon, when I crossed paths by the gates of the Jardins du Luxembourg with a man wearing a ratty Shetland pullover, whose brown hair and hawk nose seemed familiar. Yes, of course, I often used to see him in the café where that girl and I would meet. A certain François, nicknamed "the Philosopher," probably because he gave private lessons in philosophy.

He didn't recognize me. He was holding a book and he looked like an overripe student. I had returned to that neighborhood by chance, after a quarter of a century, and now here was that unchanged man, forever faithful to the sixties. I could have said something to him, but the amount of time since our last meeting made him inaccessible, like someone I'd left on the beach of a faraway island. I had set sail.

I saw him again today, on the other side of the gardens, in the company of a young blonde. He lingered for a moment, talking to her at the entrance to the RER station that replaced the old Luxembourg stop. Then she went down the steps and left him on his own.

He walked with quick steps on the sidewalk of Boulevard Saint-Michel toward Port-Royal. He was still holding his book. I tried to follow him, keeping an eye on his Shetland pullover with its greenish stain, until I lost sight of it around Rue de l'Abbé-de-l'Epée.

I crossed through the gardens. Was it because of meeting that ghost? Or the alleys of the Luxembourg, where I hadn't walked in ages? In the late-afternoon light, it seemed to me that the years had become conflated and time transparent. One day, I had accompanied that girl who acted in movies, in her convertible, from the Montagne-Sainte-Geneviève to the Saint-Maurice film studios. We followed the river to the outskirts of Paris and the plane trees formed a canopy of foliage. It was in the spring of 1963 or 1964.

The snow that turns into mud on the sidewalks, the railings around the Cluny thermal baths where unlicensed street hawkers had their stalls, the bare trees, all those tones of gray and black that I still recall put me in mind of Violette Nozière. She used to meet her dates in a hotel on Rue Victor-Cousin, near the Sorbonne, and at the Palais du Café on Boulevard Saint-Michel.

Violette was a pale-skinned brunette whom the tabloids of the time compared to a venomous flower and whom they nicknamed the "poison girl." She struck up acquaintances at the Palais du Café with ersatz students wearing jackets that were too tight at the waist and tortoiseshell glasses. She convinced them she was expecting a large inheritance and promised them the moon: exotic trips, a Bugatti . . . She had probably crossed paths on the boulevard with the T. couple, who had just moved into their small apartment on Rue des Fossés-Saint-Jacques.

A bit farther down the street from the Palais du Café, on the opposite side, a twenty-year-old girl, Sylviane, played billiards upstairs at the Cluny. She wasn't a pale brunette like Violette, but auburn-haired, with the kind of coloring you might call Irish. She wouldn't remain long in the grayness of the Latin Quarter. Soon she would be spotted in the Faubourg Montmartre, at the Fantasio, and in the billiards parlors on Boulevard des Capucines. Then she'd frequent the Cercle Haussmann on Rue de la Michodière, where she'd meet some patrons. Gifts, jewelry, the easy life, the riding club in Neuilly . . . At the start of the Occupation, she would marry a penniless suitor who nonetheless bore the title marquis of the empire. She would spend long sojourns in the Free Zone, on the Côte d'Azur, and the president of the Société des Bains de Mer in Monaco would count among her admirers. Her return to the Occupied Zone . . . Her meeting with a certain Eddy Pagnon in dubious circumstances . . . But, in that spring of 1933, she was still living with her mother, in Chelles, in the Seine-et-Marne region, and she commuted to Paris on a Meaux line train that dropped her off at the Gare de l'Est. According to a witness questioned by the detectives, one of the two women who brought the T. couple to Le Perreux had auburn hair and didn't seem older than twenty. She lived in the eastern suburbs. But was her name Sylviane?

She crops up again eleven years later, in the spring of 1944, in a small hotel on the Quai d'Austerlitz. She's waiting for that Eddy Pagnon who, since the month of May, has been bootlegging wine from Bordeaux to Paris.

On evenings when he has to drive from Paris to Bordeaux, he stops the truck across from the hotel, on the sidewalk next to the river, in the shadow of two rows of plane trees. He goes to meet her in her room. Soon it will be curfew. The distant rumbling of the metro over the Pont de Bercy occasionally breaks the silence. Through the window of the hall that leads to her room, one can still see, in the twilight, the tracks of the Gare d'Austerlitz; but they're deserted and one wonders if the station has been abandoned.

They have dinner downstairs, in the café. The door and windows have their curtains drawn because of the blackout. They are the only diners. They get served food from the black market, and the hotel manager, who was on the phone behind the counter, comes to sit with them. Pagnon makes his trips between Bordeaux and Paris on behalf of this man, who owns a warehouse nearby, on the Quai Saint-Bernard, at the Halle aux Vins, the central wine market. After dinner, the manager gives Pagnon a few final instructions. Sylviane then walks him to the truck on the Quai d'Austerlitz. The engine rumbles for a long while, then the truck disappears into the dark. She returns to her hotel room and lies down on the unmade bed. A bed with brass bars. Walls covered in old wallpaper with pink roses. A pause. She has known hotel rooms like this, when she was much younger, on nights when she didn't go home to Chelles to sleep in her mother's minuscule cottage.

She will wait for him until the following evening. He'll drive the truck to the warehouse in the Halle aux Vins so they can unload his cargo and then he'll go on foot from the Quai Saint-Bernard to the hotel. In that fleabag, she reconnects with the décor of her youth. As for me, I recall a childhood memory: fat Lucien P. sprawled on one of the leather armchairs in my father's office. I had heard them talking one day about a certain Sylviane with auburn hair. Was it Fat Lucien who introduced her to my father or the other way around? From what he confided to me, my father had also frequented the Latin Quarter in the early thirties, in the same period and at the same age as Violette Nozière and Sylviane. Perhaps he had first met her in the billiards room of the Café de Cluny.

A little past the Quai d'Austerlitz, near the Pont de Bercy, do the warehouses known as the Magasins Généraux still exist? In the winter of '43, my father had been interned in that annex of the Drancy transit camp. One evening, someone came and had him released: was it Eddy Pagnon, who was then part of what they later called the Rue Lauriston gang? Too many coincidences make me think so: Sylviane, Fat Lucien . . . I tried to find the garage where Pagnon worked before the war and, among the new scraps of information that I've managed to gather on him, there is this: arrested by the Germans in November 1941 for having double-crossed them in a black market affair involving raincoats. Detained at La Santé. Freed by Chamberlin, alias "Henri." Goes to work for him on Rue Lauriston. Leaves the Rue Lauriston gang three months before the Liberation. Retires to Barbizon with his mistress, the marquise d'A. He owned a racehorse and an automobile. Gets himself a job as driver of a truck transporting wines from Bordeaux to Paris.

When my father left the Magasins Généraux, I wonder what route he took in the blackout. He must have felt dumbfounded at having been spared.

Of all the neighborhoods on the Left Bank, the area that stretches from the Pont de Bercy to the fences around the Jardin des Plantes remains the most crepuscular for me. One arrives by night at the Gare d'Austerlitz. And night, around here, smells like wine and coal. I leave behind the train station and those dark masses along the Seine that were referred to as the "Port of Austerlitz warehouses." The automobile headlights or the flashlight illuminate a few feet of the Quai Saint-Bernard, just in front. The smells of wine and coal now mix with the scent of leaves from the botanical gardens, and I hear the cry of a peacock and the roar of a jaguar and a tiger from the zoo. The plane trees and the silence of the Halle aux Vins. I am enveloped by a cellar-like chill. Somewhere someone is rolling a barrel, and that doleful sound slowly fades into the distance. It seems that in place of the old wine market they've now erected tall concrete buildings, but wide as I might open my eyes in the dark, I can't see them.

To reach the south, one needed to go through tunnels: Tombe-Issoire, Glacière, Rue de la Santé, lit at intervals by a blue bulb. And one emerged onto the sundrenched avenues and fields of Montsouris.

The Porte d'Italie marked the eastern border of that territory. Boulevard Kellermann led west, up to the Poterne des Peupliers. To the right, the SNECMA plant looked like a huge cargo ship run aground on the edge of the boulevard, especially on nights when the moon was reflected in its windows. A bit farther on, to the left, was the Charléty stadium. Weeds grew through cracks in the concrete.

I went to that neighborhood for the first time on a Sunday, because of a friend who had dragged me to Charléty. Despite being only seventeen, he had snagged a low-level job on a sports newspaper. They sent him to cover a footrace, and he wanted me to help him write his article.

There weren't many of us in the stands. I remember the name of one of the runners: Piquemal. We asked him a few questions at the end of the race to flesh out the article. At around five, we waited for the number 21 bus, but it never showed. We then decided to walk to the center of Paris. The streets were empty in the bright sun. I could pinpoint the exact date: at the first newsstand we came across—not really a newsstand, more like one of those green canvas stalls that crop up on Sundays—I saw the photo and large headlines announcing the death of Marilyn Monroe.

After Charléty, the Cité Universitaire, and to the left, the Parc Montsouris. At the beginning of the street that skirted the park was an apartment building with large picture windows, where the aviator Jean Mermoz had lived. The shadows of Mermoz and SNECMA—a factory that made airplane engines—have linked that neighborhood in my mind with Orly airport, right nearby, and with the airfields of Villacoublay, Buc, and Toussus-le-Noble.

Restaurants that were almost rustic. Opposite the building where Mermoz would come home between two airmail runs was the Chalet du Lac. Its terrace opened onto the Parc Montsouris. And lower down, at the corner of Avenue Reille, a small restaurant whose garden was covered in gravel. In the summer, they set out tables and one could dine beneath the arbor.

For me, with the passage of time, that entire neighborhood has become gently detached from Paris. In one of the two cafés at the end of Rue de l'Amiral-Mouchez, near the Charléty stadium, a jukebox played Italian songs. The owner was a swarthy woman with a Roman profile. Summer light bathes Boulevard Kellermann and Boulevard Jourdan, deserted in midday. In my dreams, I see shadows on the sidewalks and the ochre façades of buildings that hide slivers of countryside, and from now on they belong to the outskirts of Rome. I walk the length of the Parc Montsouris. The foliage protects me from the sun. Farther on is the Cité Universitaire metro stop. I'll reenter the coolness of the small station. Trains come at regular intervals and carry us to the beaches at Ostia.

Jacqueline had rented a room in one of those clusters of buildings on Boulevard Kellermann, built before the war on the site of the old fortifications. Thanks to fake student IDs, we could take our meals, for a mere five francs, at the Cité Universitaire cafeteria: it occupied the vast paneled foyer of a structure that called to mind the hotels of Saint-Moritz or Cimiez.

It often happened that we spent entire days and nights on the lawns or in the foyers of the various pavilions. There was even a movie house and an auditorium in the Cité.

A holiday spa, or one of those international concessions like they had in Shanghai. That neutral zone, at the very edge of Paris, gave its residents diplomatic immunity. When we crossed the border with our fake identity cards, we were safe from all harm.

I met Pacheco at the Cité Universitaire. I had already noticed him a few months earlier. In January of that year, there had been a lot of snow, and the Cité looked like a winter resort. On several occasions I had crossed paths, on Boulevard Jourdan, with a man of about fifty wearing a faded brown coat whose sleeves were too long, black corduroy trousers, and snow boots. His brown hair was brushed back and his cheeks bore several days' stubble. He walked cautiously, as if with every step he were afraid of skidding on the snow.

By the following June, he was no longer the same. His tan linen suit, sky-blue shirt, and buckskin shoes seemed brand new. His shorter hair and smooth-shaven cheeks made him look younger. Did we strike up a conversation in the Cité Universitaire cafeteria, whose windows looked out on Boulevard Jourdan? Or across the street, at the Brasserie Babel? My sense is at the cafeteria, because of that airportlike ambiance that for me is indissociable from Pacheco: a décor of plastic and metal, the comings and goings of people speaking a multitude of languages, as if in transit. Moreover, that day Pacheco was carrying a black leather suitcase. And he told me he worked for Air France, without my quite understanding whether he was an airline steward or whether he had a desk at Orly. He lived in a room in the Pavillon des Provinces Françaises. And as I expressed surprise that he could be living at the Cité Universitaire at his age, he showed me a card saying he was enrolled in the Faculty of Sciences, on the site of the old Halle aux Vins.

I didn't dare tell him that I already knew him by sight. Had he noticed me as well, that winter? Was he waiting for me to ask him about it? Or had he convinced himself that I could hardly make a connection between the tramp in snow boots and the man sitting opposite me? His blue eyes gave away none of his thoughts.

The silhouette with the faded brown overcoat and halting steps had melted with that year's snow. And no one had noticed. Except me.

From then on, we met him at the Cité cafeteria or in the small restaurant on Avenue Reille that featured "Oriental" specialties. Our conversations were anodyne: he explained that he couldn't take a full course load at the Faculty of Sciences because of his job. But what exactly *was* his job?

"Oh . . . I work as a kind of steward. Sometimes on board planes, or in the offices at Orly . . . or in the terminal at Invalides . . . Three days a week . . ."

He had fallen silent. I hadn't pushed. He hung out with Moroccan students who lived in the first pavilion as you entered the Cité, just after the Charléty stadium. The Moroccans were with some very blond Scandinavian girls and two Cubans. With this group, we would go see a film on Saturday evenings and, often, we would gather in the room that one of the Scandinavian girls occupied at the Fondation Deutsch-de-la-Meurthe, a village composed of small pavilions with brick walls and ivy. Pacheco invited us all to dinner beneath the arbor of the restaurant on Avenue Reille, and at dessert he handed out presents — "duty free" cigarettes, perfumes, lighters that he procured at Orly.

Now and again we'd be joined by a tall, dark man who worked for Air Maroc and had lived at the Cité Universitaire a few years back. Pacheco used the familiar *tu* with him. It was probably through this fellow that he'd met the others. Pacheco took part in the group's merriments, its jokes, the sunbathing on the lawns of the Cité. He joined in the conversations. But I always felt he was a bit removed, though I told myself it was because of the age difference between him and us.

One Sunday evening, he was alone in the cafeteria and he'd invited Jacqueline and me to have a *pan-bagnat* and an apple tart. I was on the point of asking him about the tramp with the faded overcoat from last winter, but I stopped myself. I only asked whether his name, Pacheco, was of Spanish or Portuguese origin.

"My father was Peruvian."

He gazed at us one after the other, as if to reassure himself that there was no danger in sharing a confidence.

"My mother was half-Belgian, half-French. And, through her, I'm a descendant of Maréchal Victor."

I confess that at the time I knew nothing about the marshal. I only knew that there was a Boulevard Victor, farther on, near the Porte de Versailles.

"Maréchal Victor was a marshal under the First Empire. Napoleon made him duc de Bellune."

He had said it in a detached tone. He seemed to find it natural that the name Victor meant nothing to us.

"When I was younger, I used to go by the name Philippe de Bellune, but I had no real right to the title."

So, his given name was Philippe. We had gotten used to calling him Pacheco, and for us, "Pacheco" acted as both first and last name.

"Why no right to the title?"

"The last duc de Bellune had only girls, one of whom was my grandmother, and the title became extinct. Are you really interested in this?"

"Yes."

It was the first time he'd given me any personal information. Up until then, I'd had no reference points. The man was as slippery and elusive as his gaze. Even his age was hard to pin down: somewhere between thirty-five and fifty.

"That's a nice name, 'Philippe de Bellune.' You should have kept calling yourself that."

"You think so?"

He shrugged his shoulders and rested his blue eyes on me for a moment. The image of the tramp walking along Boulevard Jourdan in a faded brown coat came to mind: perhaps people knew him by the name Philippe de Bellune.

"When did you stop calling yourself Philippe de Bellune?"

"Are you *sure* you're interested in this?"

A few of our Moroccan and Scandinavian friends came to sit at our table, and Pacheco regained his reserve. He joined in the conversation but spoke only in generalities. We left the cafeteria very late. Pacheco was carrying the black leather suitcase that I'd seen him with several times before.

We parted company in the foyer of the Pavillon des Provinces Françaises. The night was warm and Jacqueline and I went to sit on a bench surrounded by privet hedges, which sheltered us from prying eyes. This is probably why Pacheco didn't notice us when he went out again ten minutes later, his black leather suitcase in hand. We held our breath. We both had the same thought: he only pretended to live in the Pavillon des Provinces Françaises, and the minute he was sure he wouldn't run into anyone from our little group, he left the pavilion for an unknown destination.

We waited until he was about fifty yards ahead of us before starting to follow him. Exiting the Cité Universitaire, he turned left toward the Porte d'Orléans and his outline vanished in the night. Where could he be going? Where did he really live? I imagined him walking straight ahead, up to the Porte de Versailles, and finally reaching that desolate boulevard that bore the name of his ancestor. He walked along it slowly, suitcase in hand, like a sleepwalker, and at that late hour he was the only pedestrian.

We saw him again the next day, still just as well groomed in his tan linen suit and suede shoes. He was no longer carrying his valise, but rather a small, navy blue travel bag from British Airways slung across his shoulders. Our eyes met, his as vacant as ever. It was up to me to solve the enigma of that man. Pacheco. Philippe de Bellune. Using just those two names, I had to unearth other details about him. At around that time, to make some money, I had started buying and re-selling batches of books, assorted documents, complete collections of magazines. On the off chance, I searched for the names Bellune and Pacheco in the indexes of old newspapers that passed through my hands, like a ragman poking his hook into a pile of garbage.

And so I managed to garner a few scraps of information: the last duc de Bellune was, on his mother's side, of Anglo-Portuguese origin by the Lemos and Willoughby da Silveira families. Died in 1907, without a male heir. His youngest daughter had married a certain Fernand-Marie-Désiré Werry de Hults, Belgian but a "Roman count," and from their union were born two sons and a daughter named Eliane. In 1919, according to the Social Register, they all lived in a private hotel at 4 Rue Greuze in the sixteenth arrondissement. And in fact, listed at the same address were a certain Riclos y Perez de Pacheco and wife, *née* Eliane de Hults. These two were surely the parents of the Pacheco I knew. As of 1927, judging from the phone books, this curious family had disappeared from number 4 Rue Greuze without leaving a trace. In 1953, a comtesse de Hultz-Bellune resurfaced, at 4 Rue du Dôme, and, the following year, at the same address and phone number: Pacheco (Mme de). Then, nothing.

On the few occasions when I was alone with Pacheco in the cafeteria, I ventured a question in hopes that he'd answer and fill in other bits of information.

"In 1953, did you go visit your mother on Rue du Dôme?"

That time, I saw I'd touched a nerve. He suddenly turned white as a sheet. I needed to push my advantage.

"I have no idea what you're talking about."

He was on the defensive. Why had that detail upset him so much? I thought I knew the answer: 1953, 1954 . . . It was no longer about his ancestor, Maréchal Victor. We were getting dangerously close to the present and to a tramp in a faded coat and worn snow boots who only recently had paced up and down Boulevard Jourdan. I was eager to see his reaction when I mentioned that man to him. Would he flinch, like someone who's afraid of his shadow?

Several weeks passed, during which there was no sign of him. Did his work keep him away from the Cité Universitaire? At the Pavillon des Provinces Françaises, I inquired whether a certain Pacheco had a room there. They knew of no such student by that name, or of anyone in his fifties with short hair who wore a tan linen suit and buckskin shoes. Evenings in the cafeteria, I questioned members of our little group.

"Any news of Pacheco?"

"Nope."

Already our Moroccan and Scandinavian friends had stopped talking about him. He was fading from their memories. Life went on without Pacheco: the afternoons and evenings on the great lawn, walks through the Parc Montsouris, dinners beneath the arbor of the Asian restaurant on Avenue Reille . . . I ended up thinking we'd never see him again. As luck would have it, I chanced upon two small items in a batch of old newspapers from the years 1946 to 1948. The first gave a list of persons being sought because of collaborationist activities during the Occupation. Among these figured "Philippe de Bellune, alias 'de Pacheco,' said to have died last year following his internment at Dachau." But there seemed to be some doubt about this alleged death. Two years later, in 1948, a newspaper published a small item listing indicted individuals who had failed to show up for their court hearing, and who were now wanted by the police: number 3 on the list was "Philippe de Bellune, born Paris, January 22, 1918, no known address." Which means that his death had still not been confirmed by then.

The fate of a man wanted for colluding with the enemy, who might or might not have survived the Dachau concentration camp, left me puzzled. What set of circumstances could have pulled him into such a conflictual situation? I thought of my father, who had weathered all the contradictions of the Occupation period, and who had told me practically nothing about it before we parted forever. And now here was Pacheco, whom I'd barely known, and who was also slipping away without providing an explanation.

He reappeared one Sunday night, in the Cité cafeteria. It was late and there was no one left around the Formica tables. I was sitting next to the window that looked out on Boulevard Jourdan and, when I saw him enter in his tan suit and suede moccasins—his hair a bit longer than usual and his skin tanned—my heart skipped a beat. He came over to sit beside me as naturally as if he'd left only moments earlier to make a phone call.

"I thought we'd never see you again," I said to him.

"Air France sent me to work in an airfield in Morocco . . . In Casablanca . . . I had to stay for quite a while."

"I found out you were interned in Dachau during the war," I blurted.

"No."

He sat without moving, staring straight ahead, as if he dreaded other revelations from me.

"And that you were wanted by the police after the war for conspiring with the enemy. It was back when you called yourself Philippe de Bellune."

"You're mistaken."

"For a while, they thought you had died in Dachau . . ."

"Died?"

He shrugged.

"Why were they looking for you after the war?"

He sliced his *pan-bagnat* into very thin strips, using a fork and knife.

"You've got an active imagination . . . But this evening I'm very tired . . ."

He gave me a smile, and I understood that I wouldn't get anything out of him. In the days that followed, we saw each other with the rest of the group, with no opportunity for a private conversation. He invited us to dinner, as was his wont, at the restaurant on Avenue Reille. His friend from Air Maroc was there that evening. And, as usual, he handed out "duty free" cartons of American cigarettes, perfumes, and fountain pens, and little souvenirs he'd brought back from Casablanca.

I didn't want to embarrass him by asking if he really lived at the Pavillon des Provinces Françaises. We again had occasion, several times, to walk him back to his pavilion at night and watch him go up the large staircase, but I didn't feel like sitting on the bench behind the privet hedges to see if he'd go out again a few minutes later.

One late afternoon in that month of September, while we were lying on the lawn of the Cité Universitaire, enjoying the last of the warm weather, Pacheco showed us photos of the airfield and the avenues of Casablanca. On one of them, we could see him in a steward's uniform in front of a building whose whiteness stood out against the cerulean sky. Everything was distinct in that sundrenched décor: the whites and blues, the shadow jutting out from the foot of the building, the sand-colored steward's uniform, Pacheco's smile, and the gleaming fuselage of a sightseeing plane in the background. But I was thinking of a certain Philippe de Bellune whose contour had melted into the fog long ago. His fate had been so uncertain that they thought he'd died right after the war. He didn't even use his real name. What had the life of that man been like, the one born in Paris on January 22, 1918? He must have spent the early years of his childhood at 4 Rue Greuze, in the home of his parents and grandparents. Out of curiosity, I'd checked the phone book: 4 Rue Greuze was now the seat of the Chaldean Church. They had probably turned the ground floor into a chapel, where they celebrated the rites of that Eastern religion. Had they left his childhood bedroom intact? I planned to attend a Chaldean Mass, then slip out of the chapel to go explore the upper floors of the private hotel. And perhaps find witnesses who had known Pacheco on Rue Greuze. At number 2, the building next door, a Princess Duleep-Singh had lived around 1920, and that name awakened a childhood memory: I'm waiting for my father one Friday evening, in a train station on the Normandy coast. Among the passengers getting off the train from Paris is a dark-complexioned woman surrounded by turbaned servants and several young English girls in riding breeches who seem to be lady's companions. They pile a large number of suitcases onto carts. One of them jostles me as it goes past. I fall and hurt my knee. Immediately, the woman helps me up, leans over me, and, using a handkerchief and a small vial of perfume, rubs the scrape on my knee with a maternal gesture. She's a woman of about thirty, and the gentleness and beauty of her face fill me with wonder. She smiles at me. She strokes my hair. In front of the station, several American cars are waiting for her.

"A Hindu princess," my father had said.

In what boarding school had they enrolled young Philippe Riclos y Perez de Pacheco? Who were his friends in 1938, when he was twenty? What profession was he destined for? I imagined him being left to his own devices. The war and the Occupation had finished sowing disorder and confusion in a young man with a highly indecisive personality. He must not even have been very sure of his identity, since he called himself Philippe de Bellune at the time, as if trying to cling to the only reference marker he had in life, and a very distant one at that: his ancestor, Maréchal Victor, the duc de Bellune.

No doubt he had fallen in with bad company. The article from 1946 specifies that a warrant had been issued against him and several others, including a "countess" von Seckendorff and a "baron" de Kermanor. Were those noble titles as authentic as Philippe de Bellune's? The list published in the newspaper from 1948 again contained their three names.

> Proceedings brought by the Chief Inspector, Crimes of Collaboration, against:
> 1) Lebobe, André, born October 6, 1917, Paris 14. Broker. 22 Rue Washington.
> 2) Sherrer, Alfred, alias "The Admiral," born March 26, 1915, Hanoi (Indochina). No known address.
> 3) Philippe de Bellune, born Paris, January 22, 1918, son of Mario Riclos y Perez de Pacheco and Eliane Werry de Hults, no known address.

4) Bremont, Roger, born February 24, 1910, Paris, alias "Roger Breugnot," no known address.

5) Yevremovitch, Miodraf, alias "Draga," born March 23, 1911, Valjevo (Yugoslavia), formerly of 2 Square des Aliscamps, Paris 16, no known current address.

6) Ruiz, José, alias "Vincent," alias "Vincent Vriarte," born April 26, 1917, Sestao (Spain), no known address.

7) Galleran, Héloïse, wife of Pelaez, born April 24, 1914, Luanco (Spain), no known current address.

8) de Reith, Hildegarde-Jeanne-Caroline, wife of von Seckendorff, born February 18, 1907, Mayen (Germany), formerly of 41 Avenue Foch, Paris, no known current address.

9) Léger, Yves, 14 Rue des Dardanelles, last known address.

10) Watchmann, Johannes, 76 Avenue des Champs-Elysées, last known address.

11) Fercrou, 1 Rue Lord-Byron, last known address.

12) Cremer, Edmond, alias "Piquet," alias "baron de Kermanor," born October 31, 1905, Brussels. 10 Rue Berteaux-Dumas (Neuilly), last known address.

For failure to appear at the hearing of November 3, 1947.

Nor had any of them had shown up for the hearing on February 25, 1948, as ordered by the presiding judge for the Court of the Seine Department. They had disappeared for good.

Had Philippe de Bellune really been interned at Dachau? And on his return to Paris, where had he hidden out to evade the law that was calling him to account? I imagined him slipping at night into the little apartment on Rue du Dôme where the comtesse de Hults Bellune, alias Mme de Pacheco—his mother—took him in in secret, for she must have stated to the detectives that her son was indeed dead.

Often, as a precaution, mother and son arranged to meet not in the apartment but in neighborhood cafés—Place Victor-Hugo, Avenue de la Grande-Armée . . . One evening, they had gone together to the pawnshop on Rue Pierre-Charron to split the earnings from the last valuable piece of jewelry she could hock. Then they had walked up the Champs-Elysées. It was a winter evening in 1948, the day when the second wanted notice had been issued, proof that the law was still skeptical about Philippe de Bellune's death . . . She had left him at the George-V metro stop, where he had melted into the rush-hour crowds.

Twenty years had gone by. And now, on the great lawn, Pacheco was showing us his photos of Morocco, like a tourist back from holiday. Perhaps he would invite us later on to see some slides in his room at the Pavillon des Provinces Françaises. Or perhaps I was the one harboring false ideas about him, after all. That evening, we ended up gathering around one of the cafeteria tables and I remember that one of the Moroccans and his Swedish girlfriend had danced to music from a transistor radio. Pacheco had danced, too. He was wearing a navy blue polo shirt, sunglasses, and his very close-cropped hair made him look even younger. I ended up doubting that this man could have been born on January 22, 1918.

The following week, Jacqueline and I were alone with Pacheco in one of the cafés opposite the Charléty stadium. His black leather suitcase was beside him.

"Would you do me a favor?" he asked.

He knew Jacqueline had a room on Boulevard Kellermann. Could he ask her to hold onto his suitcase for a few days? He had to take another trip for work and he didn't want to leave it in his room at the Pavillon des Provinces Françaises, as the door didn't lock: there were just some clothes and personal effects in the suitcase, of no value except to him.

He walked us to the building on Boulevard Kellermann, but he didn't want to come up. In the courtyard, he handed me the suitcase.

"They're sending me to Morocco again . . . But I'll be back next week . . . I'll send you a postcard."

He remained standing in the middle of the courtyard. I sensed he wanted to tell me something but he couldn't make up his mind. I had his suitcase in my hand. He stared at me fixedly with his vacant eyes.

"Can you do me another favor?"

He handed me a large brown envelope.

"These are my enrollment forms for the science faculty this year. They need to be delivered by hand to the Halle aux Vins campus before the end of the week."

"You can count on us," I said.

He shook our hands. Once again he raised his eyes to me. He turned his back on us suddenly, after giving a vague wave of goodbye.

I watched him cross the boulevard and follow the wall of the SNECMA plant toward the Parc Montsouris.

Days passed, then months, without a word from him. He didn't send us a postcard from Morocco as he'd promised. We stashed the valise in the closet of the room on Boulevard Kellermann. The enrollment forms for the Faculty of Sciences that he'd asked me to deliver were just an application to audit some classes. And that application was made out in the name of Philippe de Pacheco. Our friends at the Cité Universitaire didn't seem surprised by his absence: he'll be back someday, he'll bring us cartons of American cigarettes . . . But they spoke of him with increasing indifference, as if about one of those hundreds of residents that you run into now and then in the halls, and that you might find yourself sitting with, by chance, at a table in the cafeteria.

One evening, I decided to open the suitcase. At a sidewalk table of the Café Babel at the edge of the Parc Montsouris, I had just run into the tall, dark fellow who worked for Air Maroc. I had asked if he had any news of Pacheco.

"I don't think he's ever coming back. He's going to stay in Casablanca for good."

"Do you have his address?"

"No."

I was sure that wasn't true. He knew much more than he wanted to let on.

"So, he's decided to stay?"

"Yes."

Back in our room, I took the black leather suitcase out of the closet. It was locked, but I jimmied it open with a knife.

Not much in the suitcase: The faded overcoat that the tramp I'd seen around the Cité Universitaire had worn that winter, two years ago. A pair of black corduroy trousers. In one of the coat pockets I found a very worn alligator-skin wallet, whose contents I emptied onto the kitchen table.

A ten-year-old identity card in the name of Philippe de Pacheco, born January 22, 1918. The address given on the card was 183 Rue Belliard, Paris 18. Folded in four, a draft of a letter, judging by the cross-outs and words inserted between the lines:

Paris, February 15, 1954
To the Director

Dear Sir,

I am presently at the welcome center of the Salvation Army, on the barge at Quai d'Austerlitz, opposite the train station. There is a dining hall, showers, and the dormitory has heating. Last autumn, I spent several weeks at the shelter on Rue Cantagrel where I did some manual chores. I have no special qualifications, other than I have been employed since the age of 15 in the food services field (cafés, restaurants, etc.).

Here is a list of my various employments, since the beginning:

Waiter: From 1933 to 1939: La Flotte restaurant, 118 Quai de l'Artois, Le Perreux. From 1940 (demobilized) to June 1942: Café Les Tamaris, 122 Rue d'Alésia (14th). From June 1942 to November 1943: Le Polo, 72 Avenue de la Grande-Armée. From November 1943 to August 1944: Chez Alexis restaurant, 47 Rue Notre-Dame-de-Lorette (9th). From 1949 to 1951: night watchman at the Pension Keppler, 9 Rue Keppler (16th).

I am still under an injunction banning me from the Seine Department and I've lost all my papers.

In hopes that you might be able to help me.

Respectfully,

Lombard

Apart from that letter, the wallet contained a page from a magazine, also folded in four: the article related the events of that night in April 1933 when Urbain and Gisèle T. had drifted from Montparnasse to Le Perreux before returning to Rue des Fossés-Saint-Jacques in the company of two other couples. Several sepia photos illustrated the magazine page. One of them showed the restaurant-nightclub in Le Perreux, another the entrance of 26 Rue des Fossés-Saint-Jacques. At the top left, the photo of a very young man with slicked-down brown hair: I had no trouble recognizing the supposed Pacheco, despite the passage of time. The arch of the eyebrows, the straight nose, and the fleshy lips were the same. Next to the photo was a caption: "Charles Lombard, employee in a restaurant-nightclub in Le Perreux, had waited on the couple that evening."

And so the man I had rubbed shoulders with for months was not named Philippe de Pacheco. He was a certain Charles Lombard, former café waiter, who frequented Salvation Army shelters, particularly the barge moored on the Quai d'Austerlitz. Why had he left me his suitcase? Did he want to teach me a lesson, show me that reality was more elusive than I thought? Unless he had simply abandoned these remains, certain of finding a new life in Casablanca or elsewhere.

Where and at what point had Lombard usurped Pacheco's identity? The identity card dated from 1955. So Pacheco was still alive that year. The photo on the card showed the man I had known at the Cité Universitaire, whose real name was Charles Lombard, and who had artfully substituted it for Pacheco's photo; it was even stamped by the Prefecture of Police. That evening, I went to 183 Rue Belliard, near the Porte de Clignancourt, and the concierge told me that there had never been an occupant of that building named Pacheco.

The law had no doubt given up on finding Pacheco. I learned that after a certain time, a decree of amnesty had been issued for the crime of "conspiring with the enemy." In all likelihood, it was at that moment that Pacheco, emerging from the shadows, had procured himself an identity card.

I imagined him shuffling along, a vagrant silhouette. On the barge at the Quai d'Austerlitz, Lombard had been his bunkmate, had stolen his identity card. Moreover, anything was possible in that neighborhood, between the train station and the botanical gardens: night there is so deep, with its odors of wine and coal and its growling beasts, that a tramp could easily fall from the side of a barge into the Seine, could drown, and no one would notice.

Had Lombard been aware of Pacheco's past when he swiped his identity card? In any case, he knew that Philippe de Pacheco called himself Philippe de Bellune and that he was a descendant of Maréchal Victor. I could still hear him telling me in his muffled voice in the Cité Universitaire cafeteria: "When I was younger, I used to go by the name Philippe de Bellune, but I had no real right to the title."

In the dormitory of the barge at Austerlitz, Pacheco had opened up to Lombard and told him of his life. Why, on the identity card, was he said to be living at 183 Rue Belliard, in the eighteenth arrondissement? Was his mother still alive? Where? So many questions, the answers to which were no doubt buried in a file stored among countless others at the Prefecture of Police. One would also find the reasons for his internment at Dachau and his indictment for "conspiring with the enemy." But how to access that file?

And what if Pacheco had continued to seek asylum in the various Salvation Army shelters? The loss of his identity card had meant little to him. He had already been dead a long time, as far as everyone was concerned . . . Maybe he'd never left the barge on the Quai d'Austerlitz.

Afternoons, he would wander along the river, or else he'd visit the Jardin des Plantes, then finish his day by sitting in the main hall of the Austerlitz station, before going back to the barge to have dinner in the dining hall and collapse on his bunk in the dormitory. And night fell on the quarter where my father, several years earlier, had also looked like a vagrant. Except that the Magasins Généraux, where they had locked him up with hundreds of others, was not the Salvation Army.

In his befuddled memory floated a few scraps of the past: The private hotel on Rue Greuze. The dog his grandparents had given him for Christmas. Meeting up with a girl with light brown hair. They had gone to the movies together, on the Champs-Elysées. In those days, he called himself Philippe de Bellune. The Occupation had come, bringing a host of people who also wore strange names and fake noble titles. Sherrer, alias "The Admiral," Draga, Mme von Seckendorff, Baron de Kermanor . . .

I sat at a sidewalk table of one of the cafés facing the Charléty stadium. I constructed all the hypotheses concerning Philippe de Pacheco, whose face I didn't even know. I took notes. Without fully realizing it, I began writing my first book. It was neither a vocation nor a particular gift that pushed me to write, but quite simply the enigma posed by a man I had no chance of finding again, and by all those questions that would never have an answer.

Behind me, the jukebox was playing an Italian song. The stench of burned tires floated in the air. A girl was walking under the leaves of the trees along Boulevard Jourdan. Her blond bangs, cheekbones, and green dress were the only note of freshness on that early August afternoon. Why bother chasing ghosts and trying to solve insoluble mysteries, when life was there, in all its simplicity, beneath the sun?

When I was twenty, I would feel relieved when I passed from the Left Bank to the Right Bank of the Seine, crossing via the Pont des Arts. Night had already fallen. I turned back one last time to see the North Star shining above the dome of the Institut de France.

All the neighborhoods on the Left Bank were only provinces of Paris. The moment I reached the Right Bank, the air felt lighter.

Today I wonder what I could have been fleeing by crossing over the Pont des Arts. Perhaps the neighborhood I had known with my brother, which wasn't the same without him: the school on Rue du Pont-de-Lodi; the town hall of the sixth arrondissement, where they handed out the scholastic prizes; the number 63 bus that we waited for in front of the Café de Flore, which took us to the Bois de Boulogne . . . For a long time, I felt uneasy walking on certain streets of the Left Bank. At this point, the area has become indifferent, as if it had been rebuilt stone by stone after a bombardment but had lost its soul. And yet, one summer afternoon, turning onto Rue Cardinale, I rediscovered in a flash something of the Saint-Germain-des-Prés of my childhood, which resembled the old city of Saint-Tropez, without the tourists. From the church square, Rue Bonaparte sloped down toward the sea.

Once across the Pont des Arts, I walked beneath the archway of the Louvre, another domain with which I'd long been familiar. Beneath that archway, a musty odor of mildew, urine, and rotten wood wafted from the left side of the passage, where we'd never dared venture. Light fell from a filthy, cobweb-covered window, leaving in half-shadow heaps of rubble, wooden beams, and old gardening implements. We were sure that rats were hiding in there, and we hastened our steps to emerge into the fresh air of the Louvre courtyard.

In the four corners of that courtyard, grass spurted between the loose cobblestones. There, too, were heaps of rubble, building stones, and rusty iron rods.

The Cour du Carrousel was lined with stone benches, at the foot of the palace wings that framed the two little squares. There was no one on those benches. Except for us. And sometimes a vagrant. In the middle of the first square, on a pedestal so high that you could barely make out the statue, General Lafayette vanished into the stratosphere. The pedestal was surrounded by a lawn that they never trimmed. We could play and lie around in the tall grass without a groundskeeper ever coming to reprimand us.

In the second square, among the copses, were two bronze statues side by side: Cain and Abel. The fence surrounding them dated from the Second Empire. Visitors crowded around the museum entrance, but we were the only children to frequent those abandoned squares.

The most mysterious zone stretched to the left of the Carrousel gardens along the southern wing that ends at the Pavillon de Flore. It was a wide alley, separated from the gardens by a fence and lined with streetlamps. As in the Louvre courtyard, weeds grew among the cobblestones, but most of the stones had disappeared, leaving bare patches of ground. Farther up, in the recess formed by the palace wing, was a clock. And behind that clock, the cell of the Prisoner of Zenda. No stroller in the Carrousel gardens ventured down that alley. We spent entire afternoons playing amid the broken birdbaths and statues, the stones and dead leaves. The hands of the clock never moved. They forever struck five-thirty. Those immobile hands enveloped us in a deep, soothing silence. We only had to stay in the alley and nothing would ever change.

There was a police station in the courtyard of the Louvre, on the right-hand side of the archway that led out to Rue de Rivoli. A Black Maria was parked nearby. Officers in uniform stood in front of the half-open door, through which filtered a yellow light. Under the archway, to the right, was the main entrance to the station. For me, that was the border post that truly marked the passage from the Left Bank to the Right, and I felt my pocket to make sure I was carrying my identity card.

The arcades of Rue de Rivoli, along which ran the Magasins du Louvre. Place du Palais-Royal and its metro entrance. This led to a corridor featuring, in a row, small shoeshine booths with their leather seats, and shop windows displaying junk jewelry and souvenirs. At this point, one had only to choose the journey's end: Montmartre to the north or the affluent neighborhoods to the west.

At Lamarck-Caulaincourt, you had to take an elevator to exit the station. The elevator was the size of a cable car, and in winter, when it had snowed in Paris, you could convince yourself it was taking you to the top of a ski slope.

Once outside, you walked up a flight of steps to reach Rue Caulaincourt. At the level of the first landing, on the flank of the left-hand building, was the door to the San Cristobal.

Inside reigned the silence and half-light of a marine grotto, on July afternoons when the heat emptied the streets of Montmartre. Windows with multicolored panes projected the sun's rays onto the white walls and dark paneling. San Cristobal . . . The name of an island in the Caribbean, near Barbados and Jamaica? Montmartre, too, is an island that I haven't seen in about fifteen years. I've left it behind me, intact, in the blue of time . . . Nothing has changed: the smell of fresh paint from the walls, and Rue de l'Orient, which will always remind me of the sloping streets of Sidi-Bou-Saïd.

It was with the Danish girl, the evening I ran away from school, that I went for the first time to the San Cristobal. We were sitting at a table in back, near the stained-glass windows.

"What will you have, old top?"

Over dinner, I tried talking to her about my future. Now that they'd no longer want me at school, could I still continue my studies? Or would I now have to find a job?

"Tomorrow is another day . . . Have some dessert."

She didn't seem to register the gravity of the situation. A tall blond fellow wearing a glen plaid suit came into the San Cristobal and headed for our table.

"Hiya, Tony."

"Hi."

She seemed delighted to see him. Her face lit up. He sat down next to us.

"Let me introduce you to a friend who was all alone this evening," she said, pointing to me. "So I decided to take him to dinner."

"Well done."

He smiled at me.

"Does the young gentleman work in music?"

"No, no . . ." she said. "He ran away from school."

He knitted his brow.

"That's a bit awkward . . . Doesn't he have any parents?"

"They're traveling," I stammered.

"Tony is going to call your school," said the Danish girl. "He'll tell them he's your father and that you're safely back home."

"You really think that's a good idea?" asked Tony.

He gently rolled the end of his cigarette along the edge of the ashtray.

"Go do it, Tony."

She had taken an imperious tone and was threatening him with a wagging index finger.

"Okay . . ."

It was she who called information for the school's telephone number, which she jotted down on a scrap of paper.

"Your turn now, Tony . . ."

"If you insist."

He stood up and, with a casual gait, walked toward the phone booth.

"You'll see . . . Tony will fix everything . . ."

After a moment, he reappeared at our table.

"Uh, well . . . They said my son had been expelled and that I have to go pick up his things before the end of the week . . ."

He shrugged, looking apologetic. I must suddenly have turned very pale. He laid his hand on my shoulder.

"Don't worry . . . They can't bother you anymore . . . I told them you were home safe and sound."

The three of us found ourselves on Rue Caulaincourt.

"I won't be able to come to the movies with you," the Danish girl said to me. "I have to spend a little time with Tony . . ."

She had planned to take me to the Gaumont-Palace to see *Solomon and Sheba*. She dug into her pocket and handed me a ten-franc bill.

"You'll go to the Gaumont on your own, like a grown-up . . . And afterward, you'll take the metro and come back to sleep at my house . . . Take the line that goes to Porte Dauphine and change at Etoile . . . Then the line to Nation and get off at Trocadéro."

She gave me a smile. He shook my hand. The two of them got into his blue car, which disappeared around the first corner.

I didn't go to the movies that evening. I walked around the neighborhood. Heading up Rue Junot, I came to the Château des Brouillards. I was sure that one day I would live around there.

I remember a car ride, five years later, from Pigalle to the Champs-Elysées. I had gone to see Claude Bernard in his bookstore on Avenue de Clichy and he offered to take me to the movies to see *Lola* or *Adieu Philippine*, which I remember fondly . . . It seems to me that the clouds, sun, and shadows of my twentieth year miraculously live on in those films. Normally we only spoke about books and movies, but that evening I alluded to my father and his misadventures under the Occupation: the warehouse on the Quai de la Gare, Pagnon, the Rue Lauriston gang . . . He looked over at me.

"A former sentinel from Rue Lauriston is now a doorman at a nightclub."

How did he know that? I didn't have the presence of mind to ask.

"Would you like to see him?"

We followed Boulevard de Clichy and stopped in Place Pigalle, next to the fountain. It was around nine in the evening.

"That's him . . ."

He pointed out a man in a navy blue suit standing post in front of Les Naturistes.

At around midnight, we were walking up Rue Arsène-Houssaye, at the top of the Champs-Elysées, where Claude Bernard had parked his car. And we saw him again. He was still wearing his navy blue suit. And sunglasses. He stood immobile on the sidewalk, in the space between two neighboring cabarets, so that one couldn't exactly tell which one he worked for.

I would have liked to ask him about Pagnon, but I felt awkward as soon as we passed in front of him. Later, I looked up his name among the other members of the gang. Two young men had served as lookouts on Rue Lauriston: a certain Jacques Labussière and a certain Jean-Damien Lascaux. Labussière, at the time, had lived on Rue de la Ronce in Ville-d'Avray and Lascaux somewhere near Ville-momble. They had both been handed life sentences. Which one was he? I didn't recognize him from the blurry photos that had appeared in the newspapers at the time of the trials.

I ran into him again, around 1970, on the sidewalk of Rue Arsène-Houssaye, still standing at the same place, with the same blue suit and the same sunglasses. A sentinel for all Eternity. And I wondered whether he wore those sunglasses because after thirty years his eyes had worn out from seeing so many people go into so many sleazy places . . .

Several days later, Claude Bernard had rummaged in a closet at the back of his bookstore and taken out this letter that he gave me, which dated from the Occupation. I've kept it all these years. Was it addressed to him?

> My dearest love, my adored man, it is one in the afternoon; I've woken up very tired. Business not so good. I hooked up with a German officer at the Café de la Paix, brought him to the Chantilly, did two bottles: 140 francs. At midnight he was tired. I told him I lived a long ways away, so he rented me a room. He took one for himself. I got a kickback on both and he gave me 300 francs. That got me my 25 louis. He'd made a date with me for last night in the lobby of the Grand Hôtel, but at seven, when we were supposed to meet, he showed up all apologetic and showed me his orders to ship out to Brest. After my failed date, I said to myself, "I'll go to Montparnasse to the Café de la Marine and see if Angel Maquignon is there." I went. No Angel. I was about to take the subway home when two German officers picked me up and asked me to go with them, but I could see they were idiots so gave them the brush.

I went back to Café de la Paix. Nothing doing. When Café de la Paix closed, I went to the lobby of the Grand Hôtel. Nada. I went to the bar at the Claridge. Bunch of officers having a staff meeting with their general. Nothing. I returned to Pigalle on foot. On the way, nothing. It was about one in the morning. I went into Pigalle's, after checking in at the Royal and at the Monico, where there wasn't anything. Nothing at Pigalle's either. Heading back out, I ran into two hepcats who took me with them, we sank two bottles at Pigalle's, so 140 francs, then we went to Barbarina, where I got another 140 francs. This morning at six-thirty I staggered home to bed, completely worn out, with 280 francs. I ran into Nicole at Barbarina, you should have seen her get-up . . . If you could have been there, my poor Jeannot, you'd have been ill . . .

Jacqueline

Who was that Angel Maquignon, whom this Jacqueline was going to meet at Café de la Marine? In the same café, a witness claimed to have seen Gisèle and Urbain T., that night in April when they'd mixed with bad company in Montparnasse.

The Champs-Elysées . . . It's like that pond a British novelist talks about, at the bottom of which, in layered deposits, lie the echoes of the voices of every passerby who has daydreamed on its banks. The shimmering water preserves those echoes forever and, on quiet evenings, they all blend together . . . One evening in 1942, near the Biarritz cinema, my father was picked up by Inspector Schweblin and Permilleux's stooges. Much later, toward the end of my childhood, I accompanied him to his meetings in the lobby of the Claridge and the two of us went to have dinner at the Chinese restaurant nearby, whose dining room was upstairs. Did he occasionally glance at the sidewalk across the avenue, where years earlier the Black Maria had been waiting to take him to the holding cell? I remember his office, in the ochre building with large bay windows at 1 Rue Lord-Byron. By following endless corridors, one could exit onto the Champs-Elysées. I suspect he had chosen that office for its double exit. He was always alone up there with a very pretty blonde, Simone Cordier. The telephone would ring. She'd pick up:

"Hello? . . . Who's calling, please?"

Then, turning to my father, she whispered the name. And she added:

"Should I tell him you're here, Albert?"

"No. I'm not here for anyone . . ."

And that's how the afternoons passed. Empty. Simone Cordier typed letters. My father and I often went to the movies on the Champs-Elysées. He took me to see revivals of films he'd enjoyed. One of them featured the German actress Dita Parlo. After the movie, we walked down the avenue. He had told me in a confiding tone, which was unusual for him:

"Simone was a friend of Dita Parlo's . . . I met the two of them at the same time."

Then he'd fallen silent, and the silence between us lasted until Place de la Concorde, where he'd asked me about my studies.

Ten years later, I was looking for someone to type up my first novel for me. I had found Simone Cordier's address. I called her. She seemed surprised I should still remember her after all that time, but she made an appointment to see me at her home on Rue de Belloy.

I entered the apartment, my manuscript under my arm. First she asked me for news of my father and I didn't know what to answer, as I didn't have any.

"So, you're writing novels?"

I answered yes in a halting voice. She showed me into a space that must have been the living room, but it no longer had any furniture. The tan paint on the walls was peeling in spots.

"Let's go to the bar," she said.

And with an abrupt movement she pointed to a small white bar at the back of the room. The gesture had struck me at the time as rather offhanded, but now I realize how much shame and confusion it masked. She went to stand behind the bar. I put my manuscript down on it.

"Shall I pour you a whiskey?" she asked.

I didn't dare say no. We were both standing, on opposite sides of the bar, in the dim light of a wall lamp. She poured herself a whiskey as well.

"Do you take it the same as me? Neat?"

"Sure."

I hadn't had whiskey since the Danish girl had given me some at Chez Malafosse, so long before . . .

She downed a large gulp.

"So you want me to type all that for you?"

She pointed to the manuscript.

"You know, I haven't been a typist in a long time . . ."

She hadn't aged. The same green eyes. The beautiful architecture of her face had remained intact: her forehead, the arch of her eyebrows, her straight nose. Only her skin had gone a bit florid.

"I'll have to get back into the swing of it . . . I've gotten kind of rusty."

I suddenly wondered where she could possibly type anything in that empty room. Standing, with the typewriter resting on the bar?

"If it's a problem," I said, "we can forget it . . ."

"No, no, it's no problem . . ."

She poured herself another whiskey.

"I'll get back into the swing of it . . . I'll rent a typewriter."

She slapped the flat of her hand down on the bar.

"You leave me three pages and come back in two weeks . . . Then you can bring me three more pages . . . And so on and so forth . . . Sound all right to you?"

"Sure."

"Another whiskey?"

After leaving Simone Cordier's apartment, I didn't immediately take the metro at Boissière. Night had fallen and I wandered aimlessly around the quarter.

I had left her three pages of my manuscript, without harboring much hope that she'd type them. She had shrugged her shoulders when I'd said I hadn't heard from my father in five years. Apparently, nothing could surprise her about "Albert," not even his disappearance.

It had rained. A smell of gasoline and wet leaves hovered in the air. Suddenly, I thought of Pacheco. I imagined him walking on the same sidewalk. I had gotten as far as the Hôtel Baltimore. I knew that one evening he'd gone to meet someone at that hotel and I wondered what sort of person he might have seen there. Perhaps Angel Maquignon.

The only information I'd ever gleaned about Pacheco had come by chance, in the course of a conversation, at Claude Bernard's house on the Ile des Loups. We were having dinner with an antiques dealer from Brussels whom he'd introduced as his associate. By what circuitous path had we come, that man and I, to speak of the duc de Bellune, then of Philippe de Bellune, alias de Pacheco? The name rang a bell with him. When he was very young, he had known, on a beach in Belgium, at Heist near Zee-brugge, a certain Felipe de Pacheco. The latter lived with his grandparents, in a dilapidated villa on the dike. He claimed to be Peruvian.

Felipe de Pacheco frequented the Hôtel du Phare, where the owner, who had been a diva at the Liège Opera, sometimes gave recitals for the evening clientele. He was in love with her daughter, a very pretty blonde named Lydia. He spent his nights drinking beer with his friends from Brussels. He slept until noon. He had abandoned his studies and was living by his wits. His grandparents were too old to keep an eye on him.

And several years later, in Paris, my interlocutor had again met this boy in a drama class, where he was calling himself Philippe de Bellune. He was taking the course in the company of a girl with light brown hair. He was a dark young man with a spot on one eye. One day, this Philippe de Bellune announced that he'd just found a well-paying job through the want ads.

They had never been seen again. Neither Philippe de Bellune nor the girl with light brown hair. It must have been the winter of 1942.

I scoured the job offers placed in the newspapers that winter:

Several young persons needed for lucrative work, immediate payment, no special qualifications required. Write to Delbarre or Etève, Hôtel Baltimore, 88-bis Avenue Kléber, 16th. Or come to that address after 7 p.m.

I recall a Hôtel de Belgique on Boulevard Magenta, not far from the Gare du Nord. It's the area where my father spent his childhood. And my mother arrived in Paris for the first time at the Gare du Nord.

Today, I felt like going back to that neighborhood, but the Gare du Nord seemed so far away to me that I gave up. Hôtel de Belgique . . . I was sixteen years old when my mother and I washed up one summer in Knokke-le-Zoute, like two drifters. Some friends of hers were kind enough to take us in.

One evening, the two of us were walking along the large dike at Albert-Plage. We had left behind the casino and an area of dunes past which began the dike of Heist-sur-Mer. Did we pass by the Hôtel du Phare? On our way back, via Avenue Elisabeth, I had noticed several abandoned villas, one of which might have belonged to Felipe de Pacheco's grandparents.

Last night, I accompanied my daughter to the neighborhood around Les Gobelins. Heading back, the taxi took Rue de la Santé, where a café of the type that used to carry a sign saying WOOD COAL SPIRITS was bathed in green light. On Boulevard Arago, I couldn't keep my eyes off the dark and interminable wall of La Santé prison. It was there that they used to set up the guillotine, back when. Once again I thought of my father, his release from the warehouse on the Quai de la Gare, and of Pagnon, who no doubt had come to fetch him that night. I knew that Pagnon himself had been imprisoned at La Santé in 1941, before being freed by "Henri," the head of the Rue Lauriston gang.

The taxi had reached Denfert-Rochereau and taken the avenue that runs past Saint-Vincent-de-Paul hospital, the Observatoire, and the Bureau des Longitudes. It headed for the Seine. In my dreams, I often take this route: I emerge from a place of detention that might be La Santé or the warehouse on the Quai de la Gare. It's night. Someone is waiting for me, in a large automobile with leather seats. We leave this neighborhood of hospitals, convents, wine markets, leather markets, and prisons, and head for the Seine. The instant we touch the Right Bank, after crossing the Pont du Carrousel and the grand archways of the Louvre, I breathe a sigh of relief. I have nothing more to fear. We've left the danger zone behind us. I'm perfectly aware it's only a respite. Later on, I'll be called to account. I feel a certain guilt, the reason for which remains vague: a crime to which I was an accomplice or witness, I couldn't really say. And I hope this ambiguity will spare me from punishment. What does this dream correspond to in real life? To the memory of my father who, under the Occupation, had also experienced an ambiguous situation: arrested in a roundup by French detectives without knowing what he was guilty of, and freed by a member of the Rue Lauriston gang? The latter used several deluxe automobiles that their former owners had abandoned in the exodus of June 1940. "Henri" drove a white Bentley that had belonged to the duc de Cadaval, and Pagnon a Lancia that the German writer Erich Maria Remarque, departing for America, had left with a garage mechanic on Rue La Boétie. And it was no doubt in Remarque's purloined Lancia that Pagnon had come for my father. How strange it must have been to walk out of the "hole"—as my father called it—and find yourself in one of those automobiles that smelled of leather, slowly crossing Paris toward the Right Bank after curfew . . . But sooner or later, everyone is called to account.

That dream I often have of a car ride from the Left Bank to the Right, in unsettled circumstances, is something that I, too, experienced, when I ran away from school in January 1960, age fourteen and a half. The bus I'd taken at La Croix de Berny dropped me off at the Porte d'Orléans, in front of the Café de la Rotonde, which occupied the ground floor of one of the buildings massed along the periphery. On the rare occasions when we were let out for a day, we had to assemble on Monday morning at seven in front of the Café de la Rotonde and wait for the bus that would bring us back to school. It was a kind of luxuriously appointed correctional facility for delinquents, castoffs from rich families, illegitimate children born to women they used to call "tarts," or children abandoned during a trip to Paris like unwanted luggage: such as my bunkmate, the Brazilian Mello Rodrigues, who hadn't heard from his parents in over a year . . . In order to teach us the discipline that our "families" hadn't instilled in us, the administration practiced a military academy–style rigor: parade marches, morning flag salutes, corporal punishment, standing at attention, evening inspections of the dormitories, countless laps around the fitness trail on Thursday afternoons . . .

That Monday, January 18, 1960, I followed the reverse path: from the Café de la Rotonde — so lugubrious on Monday mornings in winter, when we went back to the "hole" via Montrouge and Malakoff — I took the metro to Saint-Germain-des-Prés. At Chez Malafosse, the Danish girl said:

"A whiskey for Old Top here . . ."

The waiter, behind the bar, smiled and said:

"We don't serve alcohol to minors, Mademoiselle."

She let me take a sip from her glass. The whiskey had a particularly acrid taste, but it gave me the courage to confess that I couldn't go home, as my parents were both away until the following month.

"So you just have to go back to your school," said the one wearing dark glasses and smoking yellow cigarettes.

I explained that that was impossible: if a student ran away, the punishment was always immediate expulsion. They'd refuse to keep me.

"And there's nobody home at all?"

"Nobody."

"And can't we get hold of your parents?"

"No."

"Don't you have the key to your house?"

"No."

"I'll take care of Old Top," said the Danish girl.

She rested her hand on my shoulder. We took our leave of the others and walked out of Chez Malafosse. Her car was parked a little farther on, along the river, past the Ecole des Beaux-Arts: a navy blue Peugeot 203 with red leather seats. I knew that car. I'd seen it in the neighborhood several times, in front of the Louisiane and Montana hotels.

I was sitting next to her on the front seat. She peeled away from the curb.

"Someone is going to have to look after you," she said in a calm voice.

We followed the quays and crossed the Seine via the Pont de la Concorde. On the Right Bank, I felt better, as if the Seine were a border that protected me from a savage hinterland. We were far from the Café de la Rotonde, La Croix de Berny, and the school . . . But I couldn't help thinking of the future with anxiety, as I felt I'd done something irreparable.

"Do you think it's serious?" I asked her.

"What's serious?"

She turned to me.

"No, of course not, old top . . . It'll work out . . ."

Her Danish accent reassured me. We drove alongside the Cours la Reine, and I told myself I could at least rely on her.

"They'll tell the police."

"Are you afraid of the police?"

She smiled and her periwinkle eyes rested on me.

"Don't you worry, old top . . ."

The soft, husky rustle of her voice dissipated my anxiety. We had arrived at Place de l'Alma and were driving along the avenue that leads to Trocadéro. It was the route the 63 bus followed when we took it, my brother and I, to go to the Bois de Boulogne. When it was nice out, we stood on the platform.

She did not turn right, onto the tree-shaded avenue that the number 63 took. She parked the car in front of the large modern buildings at the end of Avenue Paul-Doumer.

"This is where I live."

On the ground floor, we took a long hallway lit by neons. A silhouette in a raincoat was waiting at her door. A tall, dark man with a fine mustache. A cigarette was hanging from the corner of his mouth. He, too, was someone I'd seen around the streets of Saint-Germain-des-Prés.

"I didn't have the key," he said.

He smiled at me, looking mildly surprised.

"He's a pal of mine," she said, pointing to me.

"Nice to meet you."

He shook my hand. She said to me:

"Go take a walk, old top . . . Come back in an hour . . . This evening, I'll take you to a restaurant and afterward we'll go to the movies . . ."

She opened her door and the two of them went in. Then she poked her head through the doorway.

"Don't forget the number of the room when you come back. It's 23 . . ."

With her finger she showed me the figure 23, in gilded metal on the pale wood.

"Come back in an hour . . . This evening, we'll go have a good tuck-in in Montmartre, at the San Cristobal . . ."

Her Danish accent was even softer, more caressing because of the outdated slang expression.

She shut the door. For a moment, I stood frozen in the hall. It took a huge effort not to knock. I left the building and walked with slow, regular steps, for I could feel the panic rising in me. I thought I'd never manage to cross the traffic circle at Trocadéro. I talked myself out of entering the first police station I saw and confessing my crime. But no, it was absurd. They'd put me in a real reform school, or what they called a "supervised environment." Could I really trust the Danish girl? I should have stayed on the sidewalk of Avenue Paul-Doumer, to make sure she didn't leave. The dark-haired man in the raincoat who'd gone into her place might persuade her not to look after me. Room 23. I mustn't forget the number. Still three-quarters of an hour to go. And if she wasn't there, I'd wait for her at the door of her building, keeping out of sight until she returned.

I tried to reassure myself by tossing all those ideas around in my head. On the other side of the traffic circle was the stop for the 63 bus. Did I have enough time to ride as far as the Bois de Boulogne and back again? I still had ten francs. But I was scared at the thought of finding myself all alone on that bus, and all alone on the lawn at La Muette and next to the lake, those places where I'd used to go, only a few years before, with my brother. Instead I went onto the esplanade that overlooks Paris. Then I walked down the sloping alleys of the garden that were bathed in winter light. No one was around. I felt better. Above me were the huge windows and cornice of the Palais de Chaillot. It felt as if the auditoriums and galleries inside were as empty as the gardens. I went to sit on a bench. Almost at once, my immobility brought that panic back to the surface. So I stood up again and continued down the alleys, toward the Seine.

I ended up in front of the Aquarium. I bought a ticket. It was like going into a subway station. It was dark at the bottom of the steps, but that comforted me. In the room where I then found myself, only the tanks were lit. Little by little, in the bosom of those shadows, I regained my peace of mind. Nothing mattered. I was far removed from everything: my parents, my school, the commotion of life, in which the only good memory was that soft, murmuring voice with its Danish accent . . . I approached the tanks. The fish were as brightly colored as the bumper cars of my childhood: pink, turquoise, emerald . . . They made no noise. They slid along the glass partitions. They opened their mouths without emitting a sound, but now and again bubbles would rise to the surface of the water. They would never call me to account.

There, on the sidewalk of Avenue Henri-Martin, it occurred to me that Sunday evenings in winter are as depressing in the affluent west-side neighborhoods as they are around the Ursulines and on the glacial square of the Panthéon.

I felt pressure in the pit of my stomach, a flower whose petals swelled and became suffocating. I was pinned to the ground. Fortunately, the presence of my daughters kept me anchored in the present. Otherwise, all the old Sunday evenings, with their returns to boarding school, the crossing of the Bois de Boulogne, the long-gone Neuilly riding club, the night lights in the dormitory—those Sundays would have drowned me in their odor of rotting leaves. A few lit windows in the building façades were themselves night lights that had been left burning for thirty years, in empty apartments.

The memory of Jacqueline surged from the rain puddles and lights burning to no purpose in the apartment windows. I don't know whether she's still alive somewhere. The last time I saw her was twenty-four years ago, in the main departure hall of the Westbahnhof in Vienna. I was about to leave that city and return to Paris, but she'd decided to stay. She probably remained awhile longer in our room on the Taubstummengasse, behind the Karlskirche, and then I suppose that she, too, must have headed off for new adventures.

I wonder where certain people are today, whom I knew in that same period. I try to imagine in which city I might possibly run into them. I'm certain they've left Paris for good. And I think of Rome, where one finally ends up, and where time has stopped like on the clock in the Carrousel gardens in my childhood.

That summer, we'd found ourselves for several months in another foreign city, Vienna, and we were even planning to stay there forever. One night, near the Graben, we had gone into a café that one accessed through the main entrance of an apartment building. The foyer led to a large room with a grayish floor that looked like a dance school or the disused lobby of a hotel, or even a train station cafeteria. Light shone from neon tubes on the walls.

I had discovered this place by chance during a stroll. We sat at one of the tables arranged in rows, widely separated from each other. There were only three or four customers talking among themselves in low voices.

Of course, it was I who'd dragged Jacqueline to the Café Rabe that evening. But that girl, who was exactly my age, had a knack for attracting ghosts. In Paris, on the Sunday evening when I'd noticed her for the first time, she was in such strange company . . . And now, at the Café Rabe, who would we meet because of her?

A man came in. He was wearing a tweed jacket. He walked with a heavy limp to the counter at the back of the room, helped himself to a pitcher of water and a glass. With his broken gait, he came to sit at the table next to ours.

I wondered if he was the café owner. He must have overheard a few words of our conversation, for he turned toward us:

"Are you French?"

He had a very slight accent. He smiled. He introduced himself:

"Rudy Hiden . . ."

I had already heard that name without knowing whom it belonged to. His face with its regular features could have been a movie actor's. At the time, his name, Rudy, had struck me: it was my brother's name. And he evoked romantic images: Mayerling, Valentino's funeral, an Austrian emperor who suffered from melancholia in some long-distant past.

We exchanged a few polite words with Rudy Hiden, like travelers who don't know each other but happen to be sitting at the same table in the restaurant car. He told us he had lived in Paris, that he hadn't been back in a long time, and that he missed the city very much. He bade us farewell with a ceremonious movement of his head when we left the Café Rabe.

Later, I learned that he'd been the greatest goalie in the history of soccer. I tried to find photos of him and of all his Austrian friends with melodious names who'd been on the Vienna Wunderteam, and who had dazzled the spectators in the stadiums with their grace. Rudy Hiden had had to quit soccer. He had opened a nightclub in Paris, on Rue Magellan. Then a bar on Rue de la Michodière. He had broken his leg. He had returned to Vienna, his native city, where he lived as a vagrant.

I can still see him under the neon lights of the Café Rabe, coming toward us with his broken gait. Is it only by chance that I came across this letter of F. Scott Fitzgerald's, which reminds me of him? "I honestly think that all the prizefighters, actors, writers who live by their own personal performances ought to have managers in their best years. The ephemeral part of the talent seems, when it is in hiding so apart from one, so 'otherwise,' that it seems it ought to have some better custodian than the poor individual with whom it lodges and who is left with the bill."

Which he will settle at the Café Rabe.

I had met Jacqueline one Sunday evening, in Paris, in the six-teenth. A curious arrondissement. Claude Bernard, for instance, whose police file I'd like to peruse to learn more about the man I met at nineteen, often dined at restaurants in that quarter. The members of the Rue Lauriston gang as well. Pagnon lived in a deluxe furnished apartment at 48-bis Rue des Belles-Feuilles. He frequented the riding club in Neuilly and even the grounds of the Cercle de l'Etrier in the Bois de Boulogne, which he had requisitioned one afternoon through "Henri" so that his mistress could go horseback riding all on her own, without being bothered by anyone . . .

Rack my brains as I might for memories of the sixteenth arron-dissement, I find only empty apartments, as if everything has been repossessed—like in Simone Cordier's living room.

That Sunday evening, it was raining. It was in October or Novem-ber. Claude Bernard had arranged to meet me for dinner in a restau-rant on Rue de la Tour. The day before, I'd sold him the complete works of Balzac—the Veuve Houssiaux edition. I arrived first. The only customer. I waited in a small room with light wood paneling. Photos of jockeys and riding instructors, most of them inscribed, decorated the walls.

Three people made a noisy entrance: a blond man of about fifty, tall and well built, wearing a hunting jacket and an ascot; a dark-haired man who was much younger and shorter than the first; and a girl about my age, with chestnut hair and light-colored eyes, wrapped in a fur coat. The restaurant owner made a beeline toward them, a smile on his face.

"What's new?"

Short-and-dark gave him a smug up-and-down look.

"Vierzon to Paris in an hour and a quarter . . . There was nobody on the road . . . Averaged a hundred miles an hour . . . These two were scared witless."

He nodded toward the girl and the blond man in the riding jacket. The latter shrugged.

"He thinks he's a racing driver. He forgets I was racing with Wimille and Sommer when I was twenty . . ."

The three men burst out laughing. As for the girl, she seemed to be sulking. The owner showed them to a table facing mine. He hadn't noticed my presence. The dark-haired man had his back to me. The other one was seated next to the girl, on the bench. She hadn't removed her fur. The telephone rang. The phone was on the bar, to my right.

"It's for you, Monsieur . . ."

The owner held out the receiver to me. I got up. The eyes of all three of them were on me. The dark-haired one had even turned around. Claude Bernard apologized for not being able to join me. He was "stuck"—he said—in his house on the Ile des Loups "owing to an unexpected visit." He asked if I had enough on me to pay for dinner. Fortunately, I'd kept the three thousand francs from the sale of the Balzac in the inner pocket of my jacket. When I hung up, my eyes met the girl's. I didn't dare leave the restaurant without ordering, as I would have had to ask for my coat, which a waiter had put in the cloakroom at the back of the restaurant.

I returned to that place several times. With Claude Bernard, or else alone. Claude Bernard was surprised at my constancy in going to Rue de la Tour. I wanted to know more about that girl who didn't take off her fur coat and who always looked sullen.

Every Sunday evening, they made their entrance at around nine-thirty. They were in a group of four or five, sometimes more. They were loud, and the owner treated them with affable deference. The girl sat at their table, very stiff, and always next to the blond in the riding jacket. She never said a word. She seemed absent. Her fur coat clashed with the youthfulness of her face.

"Vierzon to Paris in an hour and a quarter . . . There was nobody on the road . . ." The echo of those words, which I'd heard that first Sunday, is now so faint that I have to strain my ears. The years have covered them over with static. Vierzon . . . They were returning from Sologne, where the blond in the hunting jacket owned a chateau and property. He bore the title of marquis. Later, I learned his name, which conjured up the wasp-waisted pages of the Valois court and Morgane le Fay, from which his family claimed to descend.

But I had in front of me only a man with a heavyset face and coarse voice. I felt an unease similar to the one that gripped me a few years later, when I overheard a conversation between forwarding agents and meatpacking truckers at an inn near Paris: they were talking about the poachers who supplied them with deer and venison, about clandestine slaughters and nocturnal deliveries to horse butchers' shops; the places where they operated were the ones whose graceful names had been sung by Gérard de Nerval: Crépy-en-Valois, Mortefontaine, Loisy, La Chapelle-en-Serval . . .

So they were returning from Sologne. The marquis was master of the hounds for a hunting rally that "unleashed"—I had caught that word from their mouths—in the Vierzon forest. The rally was called the "Sologne–Menehou Pond." And I imagined that pond at the end of a forest path, at sunset. In the distance, a fanfare of hunting horns tugged at my heart. I couldn't take my eyes off the still waters with their reddish reflections, the water lilies, the bulrushes. Little by little, the surface of the water turned black, and I saw that girl, as a child, at the edge of the pond in Menehou . . .

After several Sundays, the restaurant owner began to recognize me. I had taken advantage of a moment when the others hadn't yet arrived for dinner, and I'd asked him who that girl in the fur coat was, with regard to the marquis whom she always seemed to be with and who always sat next to her. "A poor relation," he'd said with a shrug.

A poor relation, certainly born, like the marquis, into a very old, aristocratic family whose origins were lost in the mists of time and in the depths of the forests of the Ile de France and Sologne ... I was certain she'd spent her childhood in a boarding school in Bourges, with the Ursuline sisters. She was the only descendant of one of those extinct families with no male heirs, the kind that people called "overseas half-breeds," who remained in Constantinople, Greece, and Sicily for centuries after the Crusades. Much later, one of her ancestors had returned to Sologne, their native land, to discover a ruined castle on the banks of the Menehou pond, and linden trees, in whose shade, in summer, large butterflies gently swirled.

One Sunday evening, she was being even sulkier than usual, in her fur coat. From my table I watched the marquis's attempts to cheer her up: he tickled her chin with his index finger, but she turned her head away sharply, as if she'd been startled by the touch of something viscous. I shared her disgust: the marquis's hands were thick and ruddy, the hands of a strangler that called to mind the title of a documentary, *The Blood of Beasts*. That memory joins with the memory of the conversation overheard between agents and meat shippers who crisscrossed the country of Nerval. How dare that hulking blond in his hunting jacket soil such a delicate face with his hand? Claude Bernard, who one Sunday had noticed my interest in the girl, had kindly remarked, "She looks like Joan Fontaine, my favorite actress ..."

The compliment had struck me as only half-right. Joan Fontaine was English, whereas for me that girl represented the ideal Frenchwoman, as I imagined her at the time.

That evening, I noticed there was a larger group at their table than on other Sundays. I could name names: a certain Jean Terrail, whom

Claude Bernard had recognized among them the previous week, a dark-haired fellow who, he said, managed a hotel on Rue François-1er. Now, among the information I had gathered about Pagnon, there was this: "In 1943, personally swindled 300,000 francs in German marks that had been entrusted to him for sale by a Mr. Jean Terrail." The world to which these people belonged revived some memories from childhood: it was my father's world. Marquis and captains of industry. Gentlemen of fortune. Prison fodder. Angel Maquignon. I rescue them from the void one final time before they sink back into it forever.

Today, those Sunday evening diners seem as far away in time as if a century had elapsed. All that lively company is dead. My only interest in them is that they formed around Jacqueline a jewel case of decaying velvet . . . Vierzon to Paris in an hour and a quarter . . . There was nobody on the road . . . The restaurant door opens onto her, and from outside wafts an odor of wet earth and linden.

In the middle of dinner, she had suddenly stood up. The marquis had tried to detain her by taking her shoulder. But she had left their table and listlessly drifted out of the restaurant. The marquis hadn't turned a hair. He had feigned indifference and forced himself to take part in the general conversation.

I hadn't yet started my meal. I stood up in turn. An impulse pushed me outside. I had been watching her for weeks, and our eyes had barely met.

She was about ten yards ahead of me, on the sidewalk. She was walking with that same indolent step. I quickly caught up with her. She turned around. I remained speechless. I managed to stammer out:

"Have you . . . abandoned your friends?"

"Yes. Why did you ask me that?"

She raised the collar of her fur coat and pulled it tight it around her throat. Her ironic gaze was resting on me.

"I think I know one of your friends, by sight . . ."

She started walking again and I followed along, fearing she'd say something cutting. But she seemed to find it natural that I should remain at her side. We turned into that dead-end alley lined with houses that they call Avenue Rodin.

"So, you know one of my friends. Which one?"

It started to rain. We took shelter under the porch of the first building.

"The blond gentleman," I said. "The marquis de something."

She smiled at me.

"You mean the old prick?"

Her voice was soft, slightly indistinct, and she had pronounced those two words without stressing them. I suddenly realized that I'd been all wrong about her and that my imagination had led me astray. It was better this way. For me, from then on, she was simply Jacqueline of Avenue Rodin.

We waited for the rain to let up and then we walked to her place. Straight ahead, down Rue de la Tour. Then we followed Boulevard Delessert, in that area of Passy built in tiers that descend toward the river. A steep flight of steps brought us to a little street that led onto the quay. The elevator was out of service. Two adjoining rooms. In one of them, a large bed with a padded satin headboard.

"The old prick is going to show up. Is it all right with you if we turn out the light?"

Still in that soft, composed voice, as if it were a matter of course. We sat side by side on the sofa, in the half-light. She hadn't removed her fur coat. She put her face close to mine.

"And you, what were you doing all those Sunday evenings in the restaurant?"

She had taken me by surprise. A mocking smile played about her lips. She leaned her head on my shoulder and stretched out her legs on the sofa. I caught the scent of her hair. I didn't dare move. I heard the sound of an engine down below.

"That must be the old prick," she whispered.

She got up and went to look out the window. The engine shut off. I went to look as well. It was raining very hard. A large, black English automobile was parked along the sidewalk. The marquis was standing immobile in front of the building. He wasn't wearing an overcoat or raincoat. She left the window and went back to sit on the sofa.

"What is he doing?" she asked.

"Nothing. He's standing in the rain."

But after a moment, he headed for the door of the building. I heard his heavy step on the stairs. He gave two sharp knocks. She didn't move from the sofa. He started pounding on the door. It was as if he was trying to break it down. Then silence again. His heavy step grew fainter on the stairs.

I hadn't moved from the window. Under the pouring rain, he crossed the street and went to lean against the retaining wall of the steps we had walked down shortly before. And he stood there, unmoving, his back against the wall, his head raised toward the building façade. Rainwater poured onto him from the top of the steps, and his jacket was drenched. But he did not move an inch. At that moment a phenomenon occurred for which I'm still trying to find an explanation: had the street lamp at the top of the steps suddenly gone out? Little by little, that man melted into the wall. Or else the rain, from falling on him so heavily, had dissolved him, the way water dilutes a fresco that hasn't had time to dry properly. As hard as I pressed my forehead against the glass and peered at the dark gray wall, no trace of him remained. He had vanished in that sudden way that I'd later notice in other people, like my father, which leaves you so puzzled that you have no choice but to look for proofs and clues to convince yourself these people had really existed.

Spring came early this year. It was very warm on March 18 and 19, 1990. Overnight, the buds blossomed into leaves on the chestnut trees in the Luxembourg. In front of the entrance to the gardens, on Rue Guynemer, multicolored buses stop and let out Japanese tourists. In rows, they follow an alley to the Statue of Liberty that rises at the edge of a lawn, a miniature replica of the one in New York.

A short while ago, I was sitting on a bench, not far from that statue. A man with silver hair wearing a blue suit walked at the head of a group of Japanese and, in front of the statue, gave them, with movements of his arm, a few explanations in approximate English. I mixed with the group. I didn't take my eyes off that man; I focused on the timbre of his voice. I thought I recognized the false Pacheco from the time of the Cité Universitaire. He was carrying a travel bag with the TWA airlines logo on it. He had aged. Was it really he? The same tanned skin, as when he'd returned from Casablanca, and the same eyes that were so blue they were empty.

I moved closer to him. I was tempted to tap him on the shoulder and interrupt his spiel. And say, holding out my hand, "Monsieur Lombard, I presume?"

The Japanese took a few photos of the statue, and their group made an about-face down the alley that leads to the gate on Rue Guynemer. The man with the silver hair and blue suit led the way. They climbed into the bus that was waiting at the sidewalk. The man counted the Japanese as they passed in front of him.

He climbed on in turn and sat next to the driver. He was holding a microphone. The Jardins du Luxembourg was just one stop and they had all of Paris to visit. I wanted to follow them on that glorious morning, harbinger of spring, and be just a simple tourist. No doubt I would have rediscovered a city I had lost and, through its avenues, the feeling I'd once had of being light and carefree.

At the age of twenty, I had left for Vienna with Jacqueline of Avenue Rodin. I remembered the days preceding our departure and an afternoon at the Porte d'Italie. I had visited a small kennel at the end of Avenue d'Italie. In one of the cages, a terrier was watching me with black eyes, head slightly cocked, ears raised, as if he wanted to start a conversation and not miss a single word of what I would say. Or else, he was simply waiting for me to deliver him from his prison — which I did after a few moments' hesitation. Why not take a dog to Vienna?

I sat down with him at a sidewalk café table. It was June. They hadn't yet dug the foundations for the *périphérique*, which gives such a feeling of enclosure. Back then, the gates of Paris were all in vanishing perspectives; the city gradually loosened its grip and faded into barren lots. And one could still believe that adventure lay right around every street corner.

This page constitutes a continuation of the copyright page on p. iv.

Library of Congress Cataloging-in-Publication Data
Modiano, Patrick, 1945–. [Novels. Selections. English]
Suspended sentences : three novellas / Patrick Modiano ; translated from the French by
Mark Polizzotti.
    pages   cm. — (Margellos world republic of letters)
Originally published in French as: Chien de printemps (1993); Remise de peine (1988);
and Fleurs de ruine (1991).
ISBN 978-0-300-19805-8 (pbk. : alk. paper) 1. Modiano, Patrick, 1945–, Translations into
English. I. Polizzotti, Mark, translator. II. Modiano, Patrick, 1945–, Chien de printemps,
English. III. Modiano, Patrick, 1945–, Remise de peine. English. IV. Modiano, Patrick,
1945–, Fleurs de ruine. English. V. Title.
PQ2673.O3A2 2015
843'.914 — dc23
2014026824

A catalogue record for this book is available from the British Library.

This paper meets the requirements of ANSI/NISO Z39.48-1992 (Permanence of Paper).

10 9 8 7 6 5 4 3 2 1

PATRICK MODIANO, winner of the 2014 Nobel Prize in Literature, was born in Boulogne-Billancourt, France, in 1945, and was educated in Annecy and Paris. He published his first novel, *La Place de l'Etoile*, in 1968. In 1978 he was awarded the Prix Goncourt for *Rue des Boutiques Obscures* (published in English as *Missing Person*), and in 1996 he received the Grand Prix National des Lettres for his body of work. Modiano's other writings include a book-length interview with the writer Emmanuel Berl and, with Louis Malle, the screenplay for *Lacombe Lucien*.

MARK POLIZZOTTI's books include the collaborative novel *S.* (1991), *Lautréamont Nomad* (1994), *Revolution of the Mind: The Life of André Breton* (1995; rev. ed. 2009), *Luis Buñuel's Los Olvidados* (2006), and *Bob Dylan: Highway 61 Revisited* (2006). His articles and reviews have appeared in the *New Republic*, the *Wall Street Journal*, *ARTnews*, the *Nation, Parnassus, Partisan Review, Bookforum*, and elsewhere. The translator of more than forty books from the French, including works by Gustave Flaubert, Marguerite Duras, Raymond Roussel, and Jean Echenoz, he directs the publications program at the Metropolitan Museum of Art in New York.